PLANET EVADERS

ESCAPE TO EARTH

C.T. Goodden

ISBN: 9798417628450

PublishNation
www.publishnation.co.uk

Chapter 1

Their eyes strained to look deep into the darkness ahead. They sensed that something was lurking in the blackness of night, but what, they didn't know.

They had left the safety of the Spacepods, whose reassuring glow was now far away in the distance. Now all that surrounded them was a vast open space of nothing. It was a moonless and beautiful still night, with twinkling stars above as far as the eye could see. They could barely see themselves, as it was so dark. Only the whites of their large straining eyes showed, not knowing.

It was not long after they had noticed the strange fluorescent orange glow in the distant night sky, flickering like a burning fire. No sooner had they seen them than they disappeared, possibly over the mountain range beyond. It was only when they heard the low *Boom...boom* sound far away, yet so unlike thunder, that they suspected something unusual.

Reluctantly, they edged forward, their eyes wide open, straining against the blackness of night, half expecting to see something at any moment. Their arms were outstretched, ready to touch whatever might be in front of them. Very slowly, their eyes became more accustomed to the dark, managing to avoid the odd rock or two in front of their feet. Beyond that, they could see nothing...

BOOM...BOOM...! It was louder this time. Suddenly, two bright orange lights reappeared, glowing large and fluorescent, though they seemed to be still some way off in the distance.

The Evaders were anxious. There was an eerie feeling all around, it almost felt like a heavy overbearing presence, adding further to their sense of vulnerability. They knew it would take some minutes to hurriedly run back to the safety of their homes.

The air seemed to turn chillier, and a sudden breeze from nowhere swept past their bodies. Something in the distance was getting closer and now, strangely, the surrounding night air didn't feel fresh any more. Instead there came a gradual smell, almost sulphuric, like rotting eggs. The air also felt more heavier, as if there was a huge presence in front of them, but they couldn't see and their eyes were still straining, their minds confused.

Suddenly they saw them, flying from nowhere out of the darkness, their huge, angry, burning red eyes looming closer and closer. Some were ten feet tall and there were so many of them, maybe five hundred or more.

The Evaders tried to run, their short little legs bounding as fast as they could manage back towards the Spacepods. But for them there was nowhere to hide. They were outnumbered. It was a desperate but futile attempt at safety as the giant aliens pounced like wild cats on their prey, engulfing them to nothing.

Then the hostile aliens, not content to simply slay a few Evaders, bounded quickly towards the Spacepods, a peaceful settlement for the Evaders and their families. These aliens were The Tridons – Planet Destructors - the most feared to travel the skies and they had only one mission: to destroy all peaceful inhabitants on this planet and make it their own. So, with pulsating flashes of burning red and orange laser fire flying in all directions at every Evader that moved, attention was then turned to their homes and families.

Their mission accomplished, The Tridons turned their huge, dark, scaly backs away from the burning mass, chuckling wickedly to themselves as they did so, the yellow sulphuric toxic steam rising from their overheated bodies. Having previously failed to take over the planet belonging to Tridons, The Tridons had found the Evaders a much easier target.

En-mass, they headed back joyfully to their ships, more confident now of destroying the next Evader settlement. As quickly as they had arrived, they were gone, the bright orange auras of their ships disappearing back into the starry night sky.

Chapter 2

It was another quiet evening for Zeno, who was sitting outside by one of the planet's crystal-like rock pools, the waters glistening in the moonlight, looking above at the many thousands of stars and moons that dotted the sky. Zeno imagined what it would be like to be out there, in another world, another galaxy. Neutron was a planet of sanctuary, peace and tranquillity, but nothing really ever happened here.

Zeno and the other Evaders' role, was that of Planet Eco Defenders within their own solar system, their role to help other neighbouring planets and civilisations to protect their own environments from the occasional neighbouring hostile alien species, whose intent was to cause total pollutant and environmental destruction.

The Evaders have had to defend themselves and their homes in the past. When threatened, it is only when they are able to instantly transform themselves from their average 4 ft statues, to 7ft or more in height, together with increased fast agility and the ability to levitate high and long enough to avoid instant danger.

However, this instant transformation does not last for long and their small appearance returns after a very short time, sometimes at the very moment when they need their powers the most.

Their only other means of defence, is to call upon the use of their 'Gluger, a sleek silver weapon worn on the side of their hip belts, which ejects a very powerful resin type wrap, which could temporarily paralyze any attacking alien instantly in its tracks.

Those dark days were last seen many thousand moon nights ago and The Evaders have been fortunate enough to live a peaceful existence on their utopian planet without disturbance.

Only memories from elder Evaders, told the story of attacks long ago from other hostile neighbouring planets and the battle to save their beloved planet Neutron from being destroyed.

However, Zeno was forever adventurous and curious, always wanting to search for something more. The unknown.

'Yesterday was the same as today. Today will be the same as tomorrow...' pondered Zeno. 'I just imagine I will be sitting here for many more nights, looking up and wondering what could be out there.'

Zeno gazed up at all the twinkling stars set deep amongst the dark purple sky, the occasional shimmering light trailing and disappearing, a distant firework losing its spark. Staring up, totally lost in thought, Zeno failed to notice that a few of the stars in the twinkling mass above were getting brighter, larger, as if moving closer.

As the distant stars in the night sky got brighter, Zeno could see from the corner of his eye that something wasn't quite right. He decided to wander over to his friends' dwelling, which was just a short distance away, and stopped at the Spacepod, a bubble-shaped stony white home that belonged to Magenta, Zeno's closest friend.

'MAGENTA! It's Zeno, come out and see this!'

A petite figure, very similar in characteristics to Zeno, but with larger more prominent pointed ears, large friendly eyes and the most mischievous of faces, emerged from the dwelling. Zeno pointed up at the sky.

Magenta turned her head to look upwards and began spinning around on the spot in all directions. 'What! I don't see anything!' she replied, almost falling over.

5

Magenta was forever being silly and enjoyed winding the other Evaders up.

'Look at those stars,' said Zeno. 'They're moving and getting brighter.'

Magenta stopped spinning around and, looking up, also noticed that something was not quite right. 'Shooting stars?' she asked.

But shooting stars they were not. They gradually got brighter still, and appeared to be moving slightly from side to side. The two Evaders were mystified.

'Let's call on Zula and ask!' suggested Magenta. So, a few minutes trek away, beyond another sparkling rock pool, they wandered over to Zula's Spacepod. When they arrived outside, bright lights streamed from the round windows of Zula's home, and a much smaller collection of lights were dotted around the curvature of the doorway. It always appeared warm and inviting.

Besides them being the best of friends, Zeno and Zula were also siblings, but had very differing personalities.

Zeno and Magenta both knocked on the door loudly, then Magenta rushed to the side of the Spacepod to hide. A voice emerged from the other side of the door. 'If you are selling something, I am not interested,' said Zula, whose face was now squashed up against the frosted window in the door.

'No, it's Zeno and Magenta. Come outside. We've something to show you!' The two friends looked at each other when Zula failed to reply. 'There's something strange happening in the night sky. Come and see!' pleaded Zeno.

With that, the door creaked open. 'I'm sorry...?' Zeno and Magenta walked backwards away from the Spacepod, then stopped and pointed up at the sky. 'LOOK!'

Zula wandered over and looked up. By now the lights in the sky had grown larger and brighter, their movements more erratic than before, as if they were dancing around. 'They are not stars…' said Zula, looking mystified.

'Let's call on Fusion.'

So off they all wandered over to Fusion's place that was just a few steps away. In contrast to Zula's home, it was always a dark Spacepod, as Fusion only ever put one light on at a time when he was home. You could always tell which room Fusion was in. A light was on in the upstairs window. The Evader friends knocked loudly on the door. The noise they heard coming from upstairs suddenly stopped, but there was no answer. Magenta crept over to the side of the Spacepod, ready to pounce on Fusion.

They knocked again. Now there was a loud stomping sound coming from upstairs. The little window above opened and a very irate-looking face popped out. 'DON'T YOU KNOW WHAT TIME IT IS?' said an equally irate voice.

Suddenly, a small mound of earth came flying through the air, aimed at Fusion but promptly hitting the side of the window and disintegrating into a cloud of dust. 'WHO DID THAT?' yelled Fusion, whose alarmed face was now covered in dust.

'Fusion, look up at the night sky!' Zeno demanded.

Fusion looked up, his head jerking from side to side, and noticed the bright moving lights in the sky. His mouth fell open in surprise. 'I'm getting dressed again and coming down.'

'OH NO!' replied Magenta, rushing back to the others. 'Brace yourselves!'

After more stomping sounds from upstairs, the light went out. There was a *thump, thump* noise as Fusion came clambering down the stairs. Then the door flew open.

'Has anyone knocked for Electra?' Fusion asked. The others shook their heads. 'I have to do everything myself yet again!' he moaned impatiently. So now they rushed

7

over to Electra's home that was also not too far away. When they got there, they noticed a small figure lying outside on the ground, her small body curled up as if trying to keep warm.

'Looks like Electra didn't quite make it to the front door again!' said Zula, bemused. Electra had a habit of falling asleep before she got to bed, or wandering off without telling anyone, which was forever frustrating the others.

Magenta waddled over to the nearest rock pool that lay alongside Electra's home. Kneeling down, she scooped up a handful of water with her long fingers tightly clenched, then crept over to where Electra was sleeping, ready to throw the water over her head. However, just as she went to take up attack position, she tripped over, promptly spilling the contents over herself!

With the noise of the others' laughter, Electra began to wake up, wondering what all the commotion was. 'Aarrhhh…' she yawned, stretching out long tired arms. 'Why is Magenta lying on the ground, all wet?' she asked in a sleepy, confused daze. The others chuckled quietly to themselves.

Suddenly, their moment was interrupted.

'LOOK! There's Kato and Aero!' observed Zula, jumping up and down and waving, trying to get their attention. Kato and Aero were close friends of the other Evaders and on most days, they would all spend time together, playing and exploring. They enjoyed racing on mini Whizzers, which were tiny space-hoppers the size of dustbin lids, or paddling in the rock pools with their stunning waterfalls. Some days the friends would venture over to the mysterious dense forests beyond the sand dunes, curious to investigate the strange noises that came from there. Whatever they did, they enjoyed themselves. That was the typical philosophy of a Planet Evader.

Kato was the smaller of the two friends and almost half the height of the average adult Evader, and so normally he had to rush around twice as fast just to keep up with the others. Kato also had the loudest, funniest and most infectious laugh, and a big happy face that was always pleased to see you. Once Kato was amused by something, it was difficult to stop him laughing, especially when Magenta was being silly - which was often.

Aero was just as immature as Kato, although not as loud, and although much taller, he only had one leg due to a serious accident with a mini -Whizzer. However, that didn't hinder Aero one bit and if anything, he was now even more adventurous than before, especially since he'd had a new leg fitted.

'What are you all doing here so late in the evening?' Aero asked the others. The others looked up at the sky and pointed.

'There is something strange up there. LOOK!' replied Zula anxiously. Kato and Aero looked up. They could see the strange lights amongst the many stars, flickering away and gradually getting larger still.

Kato looked over at Aero, mystified. 'THEY ARE NOT STARS!' said Aero excitedly.

'Well, whatever they are,' replied Kato, looking concerned, 'they appear to be heading straight for us...'

The seven friends stood there quietly looking upwards, the strange lights now appearing big and bright like car headlights beaming at them head on. It was as if something was about to bear down on them like a meteorite, looking more and more threatening by the second. The light was so bright by now, they had to cover their eyes.

Suddenly all around, they heard a rumbling sound, followed by a gradual shaking of the ground as if the beginning of a sudden earthquake. The Evaders now felt alarmed, not knowing what was about to happen.

There was a sudden rush of strong wind that almost blew the Evaders over, creating clouds of blinding dust as the terrifying objects above grew louder. It now shone so brightly that the Evaders could no longer see.

Chapter 3

The seven Evaders huddled tightly together, wondering what this frightening disturbance could be.

From the dark night sky above, illuminated by the thousands of stars and moons, The Evaders were able to determine the many mysterious objects now hovering above their heads in such a threatening manner, There must have been a hundred or more, large spider-shaped crafts, their surfaces a shiny black metallic, covered with bulging white lights, as if menacing pairs of eyes bearing down on them. Each craft was dominated by giant protruding spiders legs, stretched out with flat bases as if giant feet that were preparing to land.

The terrified Evaders could bear this sight no longer and they all started to run as fast as they could inside their Spacepods, clutching each other for guidance. If only they could all gain access to their Glugers – but they were all safely stored away over in the Spacepod main storage area away from their homes.

There was nowhere else to go, nowhere to hide. The seven Evader friends rushed quickly into Electra's home. They huddled together, crouching low on the floor by the front window, hoping the invaders would not see them. There came a high-pitched whistling sound and a violent rush of wind outside, as the alien crafts landed one by one.

The Evaders huddled closer together in the darkness of the Spacepod. 'Keep very still and quiet,' whispered Zeno to the others, though his voice was now shaking. The noise from outside grew quieter and the air had become still and pensive. It was an eerie silence.

'What is happening now?' whispered Zula, her eyes large and frightened in the gloom. Zeno decided to crouch up very slowly and peer cautiously out of the little window to see what was going on outside. The alien crafts had landed. They were now squatting on the ground like giant spiders poised to attack.

All seven Evaders peeked out of the window as low as they could, watching... waiting...

'*Whooosshhhh!*' A series of loud rushing air disturbed the silence; it was as if compressed air was being released. The noise was coming from each one of the crafts, producing a cloud of yellow thick steam. Then suddenly, walkways began to descend from each alien ship, at first opening upwards, then outwards until straightening out onto the ground below. The Evaders' ears pricked up in fright, their eyes wide and frightened and their bodies trembling. They could hear noises emerging from each craft, a mixture of grunting and high-pitched squeals like those of a giant boar. Then a cloud of musty yellow engulfed each entrance, as if steam was coming from whatever was inside, and then wafted out into the night air.

The Evaders still watched intently, silently waiting...

The area around each opening was bathed in light, and huge exaggerated shadows began to appear on the ground, moving along in small jerky movements. Something was approaching. The Evaders clutched each other's hands tightly... The grunting sounds grew louder, and the shadows larger still.

From a whiff of yellow cloud came movement, and large bulbous arms. Each grotesque creature sprung heavily from side to side down the walkway of the craft, until they came to a stop on the surface of the rocky ground. The Evaders lowered their heads even lower behind the window, terrified at the prospect of being seen. They could see from all the other Spacepods dotted around that other Evaders were

12

doing exactly the same thing, crouching low behind doors and windows of their homes anxiously fearful of being spotted and dreading, as to what these unknown, creatures wanted.

As the Evaders watched transfixed, they noticed that the creatures had stopped at the bottom of each platform and turned towards each one of the Spacepods. The Evaders' mouths flew open with horror, for what confronted them now was incredible and frightening.

The thing they noticed the most was the eyes. Great big slanting blood-red eyes that had such a menacing stare, as if each creature knew exactly what it was after. With loud grunts and squealing noises, the creatures quickly bounded towards each Spacepod. Unbeknown to the Evaders, each creature was carrying a weapon concealed behind its back, what appeared to be silvery in colour with a protruding tube. Each object glistened in the reflecting moonlight. The creatures pulled the silver objects from behind their backs, pointing them directly in front towards each Spacepod.

The Evaders yelled out in terror, jumping up in such panic and giving all their secret hiding positions away. Now it was too late. These creatures known as The Tridons, the most feared and nasty aliens notorious in the galaxy for taking over the planets of innocent peace-loving aliens, now had the Evaders in their sights.

Chapter 4

The Tridons began firing their weapons at the Spacepods, creating streams of hot, pulsating red and orange lights that exploded into a mass of flames on impact. The Evaders rushed out of their homes in panic as they began to burn out of control. None of them knew which direction to head in; there was no reassuring guidance or leadership, or a place of safety to turn to.

Electra's home also began to burn. Flames were now licking the front side as the Tridons fast approached, getting nearer and nearer. The Evader friends hurried over to the back door in the hope of escaping the flames. The windows and front door had been shattered, the pulsating, burning lasers now coming straight through the inside of the Spacepod. The Evaders, crouching low, were so close to being hit and were now beginning to choke with the thickness of the smoky air. The heat from the flames was so intense, burning hot like the inside of an oven, it was a living hell.

They had no choice but to risk being hit and try to aim for the back door. Clasping each other's hands, they took their chance, trying to dodge the flames as they bravely headed towards the door. Exhausted and out of breath, they finally made it. Zeno struggled to pull the door open, and as he succeeded, the flames around them intensified greatly. The heat was now unbearable, as if they were on fire. They all managed to jump out and, as they did so, they each instinctively threw themselves onto the ground in case they were on fire.

Looking up, they noticed the other Evaders they knew, all friends and neighbours, escaping as fast as their legs could carry them towards the large Trillion ships that were parked some distance away. The friends felt desperate, as their own Trillion ships were parked up behind a rock-covered hill, half a mile away. All seven of them ran as fast as they could in the direction of the ships, now joining the throng of other panicking Evaders. They occasionally glanced backwards to see how fast the hostile aliens were gaining on them.

After much uphill struggle, negotiating the many rocks, they managed to reach the uppermost point of the hill, along with many other Evaders. Together they stopped to look back at the destructive scene behind them. Their homes, everything they had owned and loved, had been destroyed in a sea of flames. The Evaders were successfully being bullied away from their beloved homeland. All that was left in the distance below was a burning mass. Now there was no turning back.

The mission of these Tridons, so hated and feared within the Galaxy, was to drive quiet, happy, peace-loving aliens from their home planets. The Tridons would destroy anything in sight and recreate the invaded planet as their own. If any aliens dared to challenge them, which most tried to, they would be destroyed instantly along with everything they loved.

The hundreds of Evaders had no choice but to abandon their homes. The night sky was thick with burning smoke and the flames from the burning settlement now lit the area all around, further highlighting the mass of Tridons clambering towards them, their weapons still firing in all directions. Many Evaders had managed to grab a few Glugers, weapons that ejected a powerful glue type substance over a long distance, that paralyse attackers on impact. However, the Glugers only managed to freeze a number of these invaders.

They continued to look despairingly at the scene below, at the total dominance of the Tridons, who were grunting and chanting all in a rhythm, as if in triumphant song.

But the Evaders were exhausted to move on. They all collapsed onto the hard rocky surface, ignoring the approaching aliens, such was their exhausted state. The Evader friends lay there still and together, their bodies breathing heavily with weariness, and stared up at the cold night sky. The thousands of stars above looked so beautiful and calm, twinkling away. In a moment of escapism, they closed their tired eyes. They could feel the cool gentle breeze on their skin caressing them, almost as if to reassure and comfort them.

Soon their moment's peace was interrupted by a gradual thunderous sound pounding at the bottom of the hill. The Evaders all jumped up in panic. Some of them ventured cautiously for a better viewpoint and, peering over, they saw below hundreds of Tridons attempting to climb up. Their attempts were slow but some were still managing faster than others in their pursuit, grunting louder as they reached nearer and nearer. The Evaders panicked even more. 'GO!' shouted Zeno to the others. 'GO TO THE TRILLION SHIPS AS FAST AS YOU CAN!'

The others rushed as fast as they could, but now they had the difficulty of descending the side of the rocky hill to reach the ships. As for Kato and Aero, the inseparable friends knew it would be a struggle for them to get back down. Yet again they had to negotiate rocks as they went. As they hurried down the steep hill, some Evaders, in their panic, tripped over and began tumbling painfully down the hill, hitting the rocks. Zeno, Zula and Magenta were more agile than the others and managed to negotiate the rocks without falling over. Electra and Fusion were slower, and Kato and Aero lagged far behind, helping support each other along.

The grunting noises from the Tridons grew louder still, and some Evaders were stopping to see how far behind they were, in the process losing their footing and tumbling painfully down.

As for the Evader friends, they continued their downhill struggle as best they could, though their progress was slow.

The Trillion ships gradually grew nearer, as long as a football pitch and a hundred feet high, with rounded tiers. They stood proud and patient, a reassuring presence, their silver metallic coating glistening in the moonlight.

When eventually they reached ground level, the crowds of frightened Evaders turned around. They could now hear the thunderous booming and the loud grunting noises the Tridons made, and they scrambled more urgently towards the sanctuary of the Trillion ships. Several Evaders tried to help those that had fallen and were unable to move by themselves. Then, as quickly as they could manage, they began the struggle towards the ships, which now dwarfed them entirely.

But, in the panic, unnoticed by the others, Kato and Aero had fallen and could not get up in time to reach the Trillion ships as the doors closed with a grim finality...

Chapter 5

As the vast ships gradually rose from the rocky surface, the Evaders looked on through the large bubble-shaped portholes, their slender hands and suit padded knees resting against the expanse of plexiglass as the Trillion ship gathered more height. They could just make out below thousands of dots, some moving, many others not. They could see in the distance fires still burning in the place that had been their home. Further away, beyond the devastation, they could make out the beautiful rock pool glistening in the moonlight and the high cascading waterfalls, which created clouds of glowing mist against the darkness. They glimpsed the dense forest in the far distance, with its fluorescent purple mesh covering the tops of the giant trees, as if trying to hold in their secrets. What mysteries lay deep in that forest they would never now discover.

The Evaders used to enjoy swimming and playing in the rock pools on the edge of the secret forest, but no Evaders had ever ventured further, due to the strange noises that came from deep inside. Perhaps now the Tridons would venture in and meet their fate.

Through the night clouds the Evaders flew, still gazing out of the large bubble windows, taking in one last look at their home planet.

'Bye home!' they said, raising their hands in a sad, tearful gesture.

As they flew further away from the Planet Neutron, they could make out the curvature of the small moons that circled the planet as if guarding over it, despite the repeated alien attacks. No longer would they be able to look up at such a beautiful and reassuring sight.

On and on the Trillion ships flew. The vastness of outer space now enveloped them. No longer could they see their home planet clearly; it had merged with all the other stars.

Zeno, Electra, Zula, Magenta and Fusion each moved away from the big bubble window. There was nothing left to see accept blackness outside. They could hear the gentle humming sound coming from the motion of the ship. They all sat cross-legged on the white floor, in a circle facing one another, holding hands. The floor felt cold, but the Evaders could gradually feel it getting warmer as the ship's heaters came on. With their bottoms getting gradually warmer, their bodies began to relax a little more. The ordeal they had been through had left them all shaking and exhausted. They looked around. Other Evaders were just milling about the vast ship, wandering in and out of rooms, around the corridors, consoling each other. Some were looking lost and confused, unable to take in what had happened to them. Their homes were destroyed, they had lost friends and loved ones.

The five Evader friends were also feeling empty and very vulnerable. Zula and Magenta were quietly tearful to themselves, for it had quickly become clear that two of their dear friends had not made it on board.

Zeno, who was sitting between them, placed his arms around their shoulders, which were quivering with grief.

'I shall so miss Kato and Aero. They were my closest friends!' cried Zula whose voice struggled to come out. 'We knew each other from when we were so small.' Zula's tears were now falling on the floor.

'Aero even saved my life running in front of a Whizzer,' added Magenta, her face full of sorrow. 'We shall never see their happy faces again'.

From their feelings of despair, the Evader friends decided to make a pact.

19

'Whatever may happen from now on, we shall always stay together,' said Zeno looking back at the others. They all nodded in agreement. The unknown now lay before them.

As the Evaders wandered around the giant ship, they familiarised themselves with the other sorrowful faces, comparing events they had gone through and what they hoped the future would hold for them. They all knew they had to find another planet to call their home. But where would they go? Many planets in their solar system had unbreathable atmospheres, or were already occupied by other alien civilisations; the Evaders could expect a hostile reception if they tried to live peacefully amongst them.

As they flew ever deeper into space, that unknown and uncharted expanse, the Evaders knew they had very few options. It was impossible for them to stay on the Trillion ships indefinitely, flying through space, as the ships needed to be re-charged regularly using solar power. And though the Evaders had emergency supplies, they would need more food and fresh water to live on. The darkness of space could not provide their basic needs. Besides, the Evaders, used to their beautiful and peaceful environment, longed to find another planet to call home.

The six silver Trillion ships flew together in sequence, and in close proximity, as if each one was protecting the others against any alien craft that might attack. Each tier-shaped ship had four levels, each floor forming a smooth rounded, exterior the largest at the bottom, the smallest at the top. The three main floors consisted of living quarters for the hundred or so Evaders on board. At the top was the control room. At the centre of it was a circle of high chairs, where those in charge of the ship were positioned. On the edge of the control room all the way was a series of control monitors, a colourful selection of hand-shaped indentations and large knobs. Smaller screens underneath indicated the gases and atmosphere of the occasional planet they passed, to determine whether the air would sustain Evader life.

Every planet they passed indicated bad news. Dangerous gases, unstable surfaces, volcanic activity, earthquakes or severe planetary storms would have made setting up dwellings impossible. They needed to find a planet similar to the one they had just left, and where there was little threat of alien life forms invading.

Through the depths of outer space the Evaders continued, beyond any distance they had ever ventured before, an unknown course of emptiness. As Zeno and the others peered outside the ship, they could see one planet pass by quite closely. They were even able to determine through the orange gassy atmosphere its violent volcanic activity.

'Hope we're not going to land there!' said Magenta, whose curious face was squashed up against the plexiglass porthole.

The others also pressed their faces up, their eyes squinting, trying to see what other things were out there in deepest space.

'Did you see THAT?' cried out Zula.

'That was moving at some speed!' replied Zeno.

'See what?' Fusion asked impatiently. 'I saw nothing!'

The Evader friends continued watching, their padded knees resting against each ledge at the bottom, their arms and hands outstretched as if straining to see something else.

WHAMMM! The ship violently shuddered, throwing the Evaders onto the floor.

'What was that?' cried out Magenta.

The others, thrown untidily on to the floor, made an attempt to get up.

WHAMMMM! It was even louder and harder this time, sending them to the floor again. The ship vibrated loudly.

A few confused seconds passed.

'BING BONG!' An announcement came over the ship's tannoy system: 'Evaders. We are experiencing a meteor shower. Please do not panic and please stay seated.'

Zeno dared to get up from the floor, and climbed up onto the ledge of the nearest porthole. With his face pressed up against the plexiglass, he could see nothing but the blackness of outer space, albeit dotted with brilliant twinkling stars.

'You won't see anything,' said Fusion grumpily, and clambered up from the floor. 'There is nothing out there.'

Electra, Magenta and Zula stayed where they were, as if sensing that something was about to happen. Electra curled up, as if wanting to detach herself from the situation and just rest.

'Come and look at this, Fusion!' said Zeno excitedly.

Still tightly pressed up against the porthole, Zeno had noticed something suddenly shoot past the ship at great speed, leaving in its wake a shimmering trail of dust. Fusion climbed up beside Zeno and peered out curiously, expecting to see something fly past.

'Did you see something?' asked Zula.

'Mind you don't scare anything off!' Magenta teased Fusion, who responded with a scowl. Just as he did so, there was a deafening bang. It was so violent that both Zeno and Fusion were thrown across the floor, colliding against the nearest wall twenty feet away.

The warm apricot lights of the ship flickered on and off and the surrounding air began to fill with choking dust from the moment of impact. Other Evaders from around the ship were also violently thrown around by the enormous bang and now some were wandering about as if in a daze. To make matters worse, the floor of the ship began to slant at an angle. Zeno struggled to get up from the sloping floor, which was now covered in dust and slipping around, managed to scramble to the porthole.

Zula, Magenta, Electra who were now awake and Fusion just stayed where they were, too frightened to move. All eyes were fixed on Zeno.

'Can you see anything?' Zula asked nervously.

Zeno strained to see outside. The others waited intensely for a response.

'Oh no… oh no!' cried Zeno 'NO!'

'What is HAPPENING?' they cried.

The others were really anxious now. Zeno seemed to be in shock, his head bowed low, his body shaking, too upset to respond. The others struggled up as quickly as they could and headed towards Zeno, almost sliding downwards due to the ship now being off its usual axis. They were now reluctant to know what Zeno had seen outside to cause him such distress.

Peering out into the darkness of space outside, they immediately wished they hadn't. During the sudden meteor shower, one of the other Trillion ships travelling alongside had suffered catastrophic damage. A huge gaping black hole in one side of the ship had left it badly crippled and leaning at such an angle, it was obvious that many Evaders on board couldn't have survived such a devastating impact. The giant ship was moving along in a slow sideways fashion, as if being pushed away by an invisible force. White plumes of smoke trailed from it, into the emptiness of space.

'There may be Evaders still alive,' said Magenta.

But there was nothing they could do but helplessly watch. Other Evaders around the ship also stared aimlessly out of the giant portholes; many were visibly upset and collapsed onto the dusty floor, only to slide downwards into the nearest wall.

The orange glow around them began flickering on and off as if struggling for the reserves of solar power.

'BING BONG.' The tannoy system came on again with a crackling sound, but nothing followed. All the Evaders listened intently, hoping for some reassurance from the ship's controllers.

'BING BONG... Evaders, we have just passed a meteor shower, do not look out of the portholes.'

Magenta and the others rolled their eyes up with disbelief. Had the controllers not realised the obvious?

'And they're controlling the ship!' said Magenta.

The announcement continued, 'We are badly damaged, as you can tell,' said the voice that sounded as if the owner had a bloody nose and was being pinched. 'We have very little power, so we need to find somewhere to land urgently, or we may float out into space. We shall keep you informed.'

All the Evaders looked at each other, their big eyes appearing wide and frightened in between the flashes of darkness and orange glow.

'What's going to happen?' asked Zula, looking at the others.

'We are going to die,' replied Fusion. 'We'll float in space forever.'

'They'll probably mend the ship,' said Zeno trying to reassure them all.

'Yes,' replied Magenta, pointing at Electra, who was now fast asleep and snoring. 'We'll get Electra on the job.'

Chapter 6

The damaged Trillion ship continued its painful journey. The control room at the top of the ship was a hub of anxious activity. It was a darker room to work from compared to the rest of the ship, which was flickering in a sable orange glow. Only the lights from the control screens were visible against the brilliant stars outside.

The Evader controllers sat in their high chairs, looking out in front of them at the huge, wraparound plexiglass window that offered a complete view of the great expanse of outer space. Other Evaders of lesser authority were frantically rushing from one data screen to the other with new information on a nearby planet, to see if the planet would be a safe environment to land on. But of the few planets they passed, not one was suitable. The ship's power levels were now running low on emergency supply, making a groaning sound as if the ship was struggling on its last breath.

The other four remaining Trillion ships had also suffered damage during the meteor storm, and were also struggling on their emergency power supplies, so they were unable to come to any assistance.

One of the Evaders turned away from one of the screens, looking grave and tired, and went over to the main controller. Stopping at the base of the high chair, he looked up at the controller with a desperately worried face.

'We have almost run out of emergency power,' he reported. 'It may not even be enough to allow us to land anywhere…'

The controller looked ahead at the stars outside as if trying to find an answer from somewhere. 'Just do the best you can,' he replied. 'And keep me informed.'

The Evader turned back towards the screens that ran along the outside of the circular control room, and looked across in both directions to the other Evaders. He shook his head. It was as if all hope was gone. They had lost their planet, their homes, their loved ones, and now this. They were powerless. They would just float in space until they all died from lack of food and water. Only a limited supply was left on the ship. All the Evaders were on strict rations as it was.

'CONTROLLERS!' A sudden shout from one of the Evaders in the control room, peered up from a screen. The other Evaders stopped what they were doing. Anxiously looking over, they hoped it was good news.

The Evader, who had fallen over in his excitement, picked himself up from the sloping floor. 'We have found a planet compatible to our own environment!'

All the Evaders jumped up and down with glee, falling to the floor in the process. The controllers looked on more seriously, as if not wanting to get their hopes up. 'Where is this planet?' they asked together.

The control room Evader struggled up from the floor and pointed out with long skinny arms in the direction of the window. 'It's just three mektrons away from here,' he replied, gasping for breath.

'Have we enough energy left?' asked the controller, her face strained.

'We are heading in that direction now,' replied one of the others.

'Hopefully the gravitational pull of the planet will help to draw us in,' said another.

'Make an announcement to the ship,' asked the controller. 'It may give some hope to the others.'

'Yes, controller,' came the reply, whose nose was covered in a white mesh, as if he had suffered an injury during the meteor attack.

The Evader pressed on a luminous blue control on the control panel. 'BING BONG! Hello Evaders. With what power we have left, we are heading for a planet with a similar atmosphere to our own, less than three mektrons from here. We shall keep you informed. End of message.'

Zeno, Electra, Zula, Magenta and Fusion, who had been resting, suddenly sat up in excitement. Other Evaders rushed over to the portholes in the hope of seeing something outside. Zeno and the others got up from their positions and did the same but, even squinting against the plexiglass, they couldn't see anything exciting.

'Look!' shouted out an excited Evader from the other end of the ship. The other Evaders began rushing over as quickly as they could with anticipation, but in their hurry, they began slipping back down again as there was still much dust left on the floor. The few Evaders that did manage to make it clambered up against the portholes, their long hands clasping on to the inside wall of the ship.

Peering out, they could see a planet in the distance slowly getting larger, as if growing. Its surrounding area was getting brighter with a pulsating movement.

'What can you see?' shouted out Zeno from the other end of the ship.

'We don't know yet but it looks good!' the reply came.

As the distant planet grew gradually larger, the Evaders could begin to determine its colours, a magnificent contrast of blues and greens. Then, as the Trillion ship reached nearer, the Evaders were able to see stunning outlines covering the planet's surface.

In the control room, there was nervousness. The Evaders' assumption was correct that the planet they were approaching had a gravitational pull, which helped to draw them in, as the ship probably wouldn't have made it otherwise.

There was much excited anticipation amongst the Evaders generally.

They were running around in all directions, slipping and sliding everywhere like children in a playground. This undiscovered planet was to be their new home.

Peering out through the large portholes of the ship, the Evaders were able to see the stunning blues of the ocean. It was a beautiful, welcoming sight.

Meanwhile, in the control room, the controllers watched anxiously through the 360-degree plexiglass windows of the ship, gazing at the surrounding planet glowing around them. What appeared to be land showed a dark contrast against a lighter shade of blue that reminded them of their old home planet, except that their waters were of a luminous turquoise and crystal-like clarity.

'Reduce speed, proceed slow' said one of the controllers firmly.

They looked out intently, nervous of what may lie ahead. All they could see now were clouds - white fluffy clouds, creating a blanket unlike the clouds on the Planet Neutron which were a haziness of wispy reds and pinks.

Everyone watched transfixed as they flew through the white fluffiness. Whether this planet was hostile or not, empty or occupied, they knew they had no choice now but to stay.

'Ohhhh!' sighed Zeno, whose face was pressed up closely against the porthole, along with every other Evader on board.

'Look at that!' said Zula amazed.

'Is this our new home then?' asked Magenta curiously.

'It's probably full of Tridons,' said Fusion grumpily, shaking his head and moving away from the portholes, uninterested. In a rare moment of anticipation, Electra joined the others who were watching, mesmerised by this new world outside that was yet to be discovered.

'Do you think they will be friendly?' asked Electra, looking around at the others.

The Evader friends looked at one another in silence. Suddenly the prospect of more hostile aliens overshadowed their temporary enthusiasm. Zeno turned away from the large porthole, breaking the silence.

'OH NO!' he cried, suddenly looking terrified and pointing out of the porthole, one hand against his open mouth. The other Evaders also looked reluctantly out of the portholes.

'ARRGHHH!' they all cried in horrified chorus.

It was an alien the size of a mountain and it was looking straight at them!

Chapter 7

There was pandemonium in the control room of the Trillion ship as the gigantic alien stood huge and still, its presence a powerful sight. 'Have the laser blasts at the ready!' ordered the chief controller loudly.

'Creature has not moved yet, sir,' said one of the Evaders, nervously studying the huge presence through the control room, waiting for further instructions.

'NO WAIT! IT MOVED!

The controller almost jumped up from his seat in alarm.

'Evaders at the ready please. Point lasers. DON'T PANIC, EVADERS! Hold... FIRE!'

With that a huge red beam of light shot from a protruding metallic funnel at the bottom of the ship, and hurled at great speed towards the mountainous figure.

'BOOM!'

A huge explosion followed the shock wave jolting each of the Trillion ships. As the Evaders stared transfixed, bracing themselves for something further to happen, they expected the target, this huge alien being, to explode into a jelly type mush. Instead and to their amazement and horror, thousands of meteorites began flying towards the Trillion ship with such force, exploding against the tough exterior of the ship on impact and making it rumble like an earthquake inside. The Evaders, terrified, tried to steady themselves against the violently shaking floor beneath them, yet at the same time their anticipation to look outside was strong, as they wanted to see what was happening. Those that managed to scramble against the portholes could see the mountain-high alien collapse into two enormous main pieces, as if the whole structure had been sliced vertically in two.

Unbeknown to the Evaders, they had just destroyed one of the greatest structures symbolising world peace that has ever been created, the Christ the Redeemer statue in Brazil. The entire mountainside was occupied by inhabitants of this planet, sightseers and holidaymakers, taking in the amazing view from the enormous mountain, enjoying the sights across the city of Rio de Janeiro and the beautiful sweeping bay beyond full of boats and ships. Little had they expected such a terrifying sight.

Two huge boulders began to tumble down both sides of the mountain, almost in slow motion, paralysing everyone that could see what was happening. Many were unable to escape out of the path of mass falling rock. People in cable cars that ran up and down the top of the mountainside looked up in complete horror as they viewed the enormous boulders crashing down, destroying everything in their path. The cable cars rocked violently from side and collided with the thick cables that held the entire cable car system up, creating terror for those on board. The two mountainous rocks tumbled down the rest of the sharp sides of the cone-shaped mountain, crashing at the base with such force that they created enormous craters, and continued in a bouncing fashion towards those below that stood in their path. Devastation now lay all around.

If the Evaders had wanted to make a quiet, subtle entrance to their new home planet, this was not the way they'd intended to do it. They looked on horrified at the destruction below. Little did they realise that the huge mountainous figure that had loomed in front of them was no hostile alien being, a living breathing monstrosity, but a towering figure of peace and harmony. But peace and harmony were not the first impressions made on this new planet by the Evaders…

31

The stunned silence inside the control room was abruptly interrupted.

'MASTER! Spaceships approaching fast ahead!' shouted out one of the Controllers, jumping away with alarm from one of the control screens.

The Evader controller quickly composed themselves into immediate action.

'Evaders station at the ready - WE GO!'

'WHOOSSSHH!' Leaving the scene of devastation below, the ship suddenly sped off, with the other four Trillion ships following closely in pursuit. Unfortunately for them, also in hot pursuit were navy fighter jets, zooming in on their tail.

'Go faster, go faster!' ordered the Evader controller.

'We are at full power, master,' replied a sweaty-faced Evader.

The long and arduous journey through space from their home planet had exhausted most of the power supply each of the ships had left. They flew at low attitude as fast as they could manage, with the series of alien fighter jets in hot pursuit.

Over the expanse of sky, the chase continued. The Trillion ships struggled to fly on, almost limping in comparison to their normal zooming speed, and the fighter jets hung closely on their tails. The Trillion ships flew in a zig-zag fashion, as if trying to shake them off. The control tower listened intently to each comment made by the fighter pilots in their overawed excitement.

'WOW! You should see them go,' reported one of the pilots, struggling to keep up.

'WE'LL LOOSE THEM!' shouted another, struggling with the controls to try to keep up with the erratic movements of the Trillion ships like an excited child playing an arcade game.

At such speed, they continued to fly over towns below; many of the residents had already tuned in to the latest news channels beaming this extraordinary race across the sky live on TV, as witnessed by helicopters from zone to zone.

The Evaders had unknowingly invaded a planet which was insular in its existence and for whom space travel was very limited, hence the inhabitants' fascination. This was the day this planet had been waiting a long time for.

The high-speed chase across the sky continued over the towns, until below them appeared a barren landscape, a vast expanse of desert leading up to some mountains in the distance. The atmosphere on board the Trillion ships was tense.

'We are quickly losing power, master, we need to land,' said a sweaty-faced Evader at the control panels, his face contorted with worry.

'What lies ahead of us?' asked the master controller loudly.

The sweaty-faced Evader turned back towards the various screens, his head moving in all directions as he studied the information on each one. He turned back around, looking even more worried than before. 'Mountains, master. There is nowhere for us to land.'

Suddenly, all the anxious activity in the control room stopped. There was a hushed silence amongst the Evaders as they all hurried towards the master controllers seated high above on the circular platform. They waited for a reassuring response. Surely, they would find somewhere safe to land and escape the chasing aliens?

'Code ten alert. Prepare for crash landing!' came a loud response from the master controller. All the Evaders panicked as the ship's high-pitched alarm suddenly rang every other second through the entire body of the big ship, and with each deafening alarm sound came a flash of red light between a second of darkness. With each red flash, only chaos could be seen as the Evaders ran around the control room and the entire ship as if all sense had been finally lost. The Evaders weren't used to experiencing a crisis, and this was certainly a crisis.

Well below the level of the control room at the heart of the ship were Zeno, Zula, Electra, Magenta and Fusion. All around them, between the flashes of red light, they could see all the other Evaders running frantically around, little screams coming from their mouths and their long arms waving in the air, displaying total panic. The Evader friends huddled frightened together on the edge of the floor and braced themselves for the inevitable crash that would probably kill them all. No announcement came over the tannoy system. No reassuring words from the ship's controllers, as they would have hoped. Yet again, their little innocent lives were in danger, and this time, there would be no escape.

Chapter 8

The pilots' view from the chasing fighter jets was astounding. Looking intently as they erratically chased the UFOs, they couldn't help but notice a sudden drop of altitude that these mysterious large objects had made. High above their heads and all around, the pilots were surrounded by beautiful clear blue skies. But down below, now at very close proximity, and for miles and miles beyond, were snow-covered treacherous mountain terrain.

What began to worry the pilots was the UFOs' erratic flying, and the fact that these large alien ships were now moving from side to side, and up and down, as if they were veering out of control. But most worryingly was how close to the snowy mountains they were now flying. A sudden movement from one of the UFOs could send it crashing down into the deep gorges below.

As the pilots kept radioing through to the control tower, there was as much excitement and tension from the ground crews as from those in the air. From a safe enough distance and again flying at a low level, high-powered news helicopters continued their exclusive pursuit, filming and relaying each detail to the world outside, albeit at a less erratic pace.

'We're going to end up with another Roswell on our hands!' one fighter pilot radioed back to the control tower.

'Copy that,' replied the control tower. 'What's the situation now? Over.'

The pilot surveyed the landscape once more. 'There's nowhere for these things to land... mountains all over.

They're going to crash. Do I have permission to shoot.? Over.'

No immediate response followed for a few long seconds. There was much deliberation going on, many were unsure what to do in this situation. The military personnel in the control room were stressed, further filling the air with tension. Then the response came.

'Echo One - do you copy? Do I have permission to shoot the target down.? Over.'

The orders were given through to the thirty or so fighter jets that had now joined the fast paced pursuit of the distressed Trillion ships.

'All stations. Lock on to target 001' instructed the control tower.' 001 was the nearest Trillion ship to the fighter jet. Of all the UFOs, this one was the furthest behind and appeared to have the least power. Unlike the other Trillion ships, which were moving erratically from side to side, 001 continued at a steady but more sluggish pace, and struggled to keep up with the others.

The chief fighter pilot in the group of other jets instructed the others to lock on their targets as confirmed by the control tower. 'Positions ready. Aim.... lock... FIRE!'

WHOOOSSH! From each of the fighter jets, missiles flew at tremendous speed in a synchronized fashion towards target 001. Within just a few tense seconds, there was an incredible huge ball of red and orange and a deafening boom, the shock wave creating a sudden jolt within the cockpits of the fighter jets as they swooped higher to avoid the burning mass ahead of them.

'Control tower to Eagle one. Can you see anything?'

The chief pilot's eyes were transfixed on what was now a bubble-like cloud of black and grey smoke below the aircraft as it circled steeply above. The other fighter jets swooped around, all eyes focused to see what inevitable damage had been done to the huge UFO.

Suddenly, out of the enormous cloud of smoke, they could make out a massive polished silvery grey surface, smooth and rounded at the edges, and as the sun's rays reflected off the surface, it almost blinded the pilots.

'Echo One to base. Object appears to be untouched.'

But as they stared further at the scene below, they noticed that the giant craft was badly listing to one side, with black smoke billowing from its side.

'Echo One to base. Object badly damaged. IT'S GOING DOWN! IT'S GOING DOWN!'

The giant smoking mass listed even further to one side almost at a 90-degree angle as it began its slow descent towards the snowy mountain range below. It was an awful sight for the pilots, very surreal, as if they were watching a tragic film scene, but wanting to press the stop button.

The fighter pilots continued to fly a tight circle around the falling mass, bracing themselves for the inevitable impact.

'This can't be happening!' radioed one pilot, his voice wavering.

As the pilots looked on transfixed, they failed to notice that the remaining four ships containing the Evaders had continued their frantic escape. They were still flying low over the mountainous region, getting slower and slower as their solar power ran out, almost ready to collapse onto the treacherous terrain below.

For a second, the pilots closed their eyes. They didn't want to see. Then... BOOM! A noise so deafening, the vibration shook the fighter jets, as if a wave of energy suddenly engulfed them. They looked down below. What had been a beautiful snow- covered mountain region was now darkened, as black wreckage lay strewn over a huge area, probably ten miles or more in radius. The whole mountain was on fire. Black smoke billowed up into the clear blue sky and into the path of the fighter jets.

'It's... it's gone,' radioed Echo One, his voice trembling.

'Control tower to Echo One. Where are the other UFOs?

Each of the pilots was suddenly shaken out of their subdued state, as if being abruptly woken from a bad dream. As highly professional as they were, they hadn't experienced anything like this.

They looked at the surrounding sky. It was empty. They could see nothing on the horizon.

'Echo One to control. They're gone. Repeat. THEY ARE GONE!'

Chapter 9

As the four remaining Trillion ships continued their frantic, albeit slow journey, they realised the devastating impact the other Trillion ship had suffered. In the control room of each of the giant ships, the highly sophisticated monitors in front of them indicated exactly what had happened. They also had a firm visual on the large plasma screen, which showed each of the four ships the horrific explosion. The Evaders were beside themselves with grief as their fellow friends were no more. Again the Evader race had done nothing to hurt others, and as if they hadn't gone through enough, more innocent lives had now been lost. Furthermore, their concerns of hostility on this planet had been confirmed. It was obviously inhabited by an alien race similar to the Tridons, who lived their lives by violating others. When would their pain end...?

From the very moment the other Trillion ship had suffered its devastating blow, the fighter pilots had been circling the area, almost as if in a temporary daze. Whatever military experience they had still couldn't prepare anyone for such a terrible sight. Although their concentration on the remaining ships had lapsed for just minutes, it had given the other Trillion ships a chance to disappear as quickly as they could from the enemy fire.

'Echo One to control tower. We have lost visual. Repeat. We have lost visual.' Composure restored, the pilots waited for radar contact.

'Control tower to Echo One. We have a visual on our screen - head due west.'

'Copy that. On our way!' Their deadly mission was back on.

It didn't take very long for the 600 mph fighter jets to see small reflective glows of light on the horizon - a set of four perfectly identical shiny objects. As the jets got nearer, the UFOs grew more distinctive in shape and colour: brilliantly silver and reflective against the sunlight, almost blinding the pilots, who had to pull their protective visors down. It was a stunning sight.

At the control tower base, there was an excited air of anticipation. By now, more military personnel had gathered, the darkly-lit control room filled with air traffic control screens, so many different red, green and white little lights dotted about, some flashing. The air traffic controllers were a collection of about twenty tense military personnel, most of them displaying immaculate rows of medals on the breasts of their uniforms. It was clear that this was a select, high-profile ensemble and the circumstances they were facing were top secret.

Suddenly the door flew open and the room went uncomfortably quiet. A bald, very tall heavy man, his puffed-out chest displaying a large assortment of coloured strips, entered the tense room, surrounded by yet another small group of personnel in similarly smart uniforms. He walked heavily over to the area of the control screens, his personnel brushing aside the other authority figures in the room. He stopped at the screens. Everyone abruptly saluted.

'General Storm, SIR!' The response from the personnel directly standing around the air traffic control screen was brisk.

'What is the situation?'

'We have shot down one, sir, and we have a visual on four more. We are pursuing now!'

'You make sure they don't get away. Shoot them down, but I want whatever is in those ships ALIVE!' the General bellowed.

'YES SIR!' came the reply, the man saluting nervously again.

The fighter pilots' pursuit continued as they anxiously awaited orders from ground control. The four giant Trillion ships continued, now travelling at a slower pace than before, zig-zagging from side to side, up and down as if trying to shake off these hostile aliens.

Still they flew over an endless mountainous region so vast it seemed to go on forever, although unbeknown to the Evaders, beyond the horizon was a massive expanse of the Bay of Driscol, its depths in places 2 miles or more. Both the fighter pilots and those in the military control room knew what was ahead. They had to take action with the spaceships now or they might lose their chance to shoot down and capture anything on board.

'We'll have to act now sir or we will lose them!' said one of the military personnel rather nervously to General Storm, before quickly turning back towards the screens in his chair.

With a bright red face, General Storm swung the man's chair around, bellowing: 'I GIVE THE ORDERS AROUND HERE!'

Regaining his serious composure, and straightening his tie with his enormous hairy hand, he gave the order: 'LET'S BLOW THOSE THINGS OUT OF THE SKY!'

A hive of activity suddenly filled the control room as the orders were given straight through to the fighter pilots who were ready and waiting.

At this moment, the activity in the Trillion ships' control rooms was just as tense. The army of menacing alien craft was outside. The Evaders looked worried and they had every reason to be.

'We cannot go any faster, master.'

41

The master controllers sat in their high chairs, shaking their heads. They knew the end was imminent. They would end up like the other Trillion ship.

'Let all Evaders prepare,' said the chief controller.

BING BONG. The tannoy system came alive. 'Evaders, there is no escape. On orders from the masters, we must close our eyes and pray.'

Zeno, Zula, Magenta, Electra and Fusion once again faced the one thing they feared most: certain death. They cuddled closely together low on the white shiny floor, quietly huddled against the wall of the ship, the surrounding lights now a flickering dim orange as the ship tried to conserve what energy it had left. Between the flashes of pulsing light, they could see the other Evaders around them doing exactly the same. They huddled together in small groups for comfort, silent and shaking. Many closed their eyes, bracing themselves for the inevitable impact that would finally end this torment.

'Zeno, I'm frightened,' said Zula.

Electra looked more vulnerable than ever, and huddled even closer to Zeno for comfort, shaking quite considerably.

'Don't be scared, Electra, close your eyes and go to sleep.' Zeno whispered. Electra looked up with pitiful big eyes.

'Make them go away, Zeno!'

Even Fusion, always the one to scoff at any situation and never inclined to show any Evader emotion, sat motionless, his long arms wrapped around his raised knees as if in self-comfort.

Just then, Magenta suddenly jumped up and looked out of the large portholes above their heads. 'Oh… I can see them, all lined up. So many of them.'

Zeno reached up and yanked at the bottom of Magenta's trousers, almost pulling them off and almost exposing the top of a rather large bottom.

'OH NO!' cried out Magenta.

A huge explosion suddenly rocked the ship. Magenta was instantly thrown across the expanse of shiny white floor, colliding against a pile of Evaders, who were also thrown violently to one side.

The pulsing lights flickered then went out, leaving nothing but darkness, except from a light orange hue coming from each of the portholes. The ship began to list at a 45-degree angle. Evaders began to slide to one side, their cries resounding through the ship.

Zeno, Electra, Zula and Fusion stretched out their long arms as if in protection, knowing the other Evaders, including Magenta, were now sliding towards them. They could hear their hands squeaking against the slope of the slippery floor as if trying to stop themselves from travelling down a slide.

The Trillion ship had been severely hit by a barrage of missiles and was now falling towards the mountainous, snow-covered region. The impact would shatter the ship into a million pieces.

In the control room at the top of the crippled ship, the Evader controllers struggled in vain to regain some power and stability. The task was made more difficult by the sloping floor. They tried desperately to steer the ship towards a flatter plain below, but to their dismay the ship was out of control: too much damage had been sustained.

Unlike the other portholes around the ship that had been frosted over by a light orange hue, as the power went, the 360-degree window at the top of the ship was left unaffected, as it had been designed for just such emergency situations. Due to the ship still falling at a 45-degree angle, the master controllers were wedged against one side of their high chairs, unable to move, the top halves of their bodies at a totally different angle to their lower halves. Whether they liked it or not, from their viewpoint, even at this angle, they could clearly see the snowy mountains and jagged rocks looming below. The ship itself was falling, slowly, gracefully, as if gradually going to sleep.

But then, as the ship descended further, a huge mountainous black hole opened up beneath them. The other Evaders couldn't see what it was they were falling into; they just braced themselves, terrified of the inevitable crash and break-up of the ship. This time there was no escape. All the Evaders now began to cry out, panicked and frightened, as the inside of the ship grew darker and darker, the blackness covering them as the daylight above began to slowly disappear.

Now they were inside the immense black hole. Zeno and the other Evaders, huddled tightly together, now nothing but blackness around them, almost suffocating. The air was much colder now that the light was gone. They felt as though they were being buried alive. They could only feel their little bodies pressed against each other, helpless as they tried to keep warm, or just find some comfort.

You could hear the cries of the Evaders as they asked each other what was happening. But there came no answer.

'Zeno. Are we going to die?' asked Zula, clasping Zeno's arm tightly.

'Don't worry,' replied Zeno quietly, trying to reassure his friend. 'We will think of something.'

Suddenly they felt the cold ship against them begin to shake with an unnerving rumbling sound. They began screaming in their little exhausted voices, then… CRASH!

The shaking stopped. The cries of the Evaders stopped.

Chapter 10

Inside the ship, a deathly silence reigned. The air all around began to fill with choking dust. The Evaders lay collapsed, quiet and still, in a shocked state, for a moment not knowing whether they were dead or alive. Some began to cough and splutter, but out of the still darkness, there soon came a reassuring noise.

Suddenly, there was a brief flickering of a light, and then it went out. For two short seconds, Zula's eyes opened, revealing the surroundings before the blackness returned. The Evaders lay on the floor; only a few were stirring, as if they too had been woken by the light. But most disturbingly, Zula in that split second noticed that Zeno, Electra, Magenta and Fusion lay motionless.

'Oh no, oh no!' moaned Zula quietly, and began to take deep breaths. She began to cry, feeling so alone and helpless. 'I want to be with my friends...'

With eyes closed tightly shut and body curled up for self-comfort, Zula saw the light suddenly return, flickering again, but this time it managed to stay on. Her eyes opened and hope returned. Zula then sat up from the cold dusty floor and tried to shake each one of her friends awake. It was an agonising moment but slowly their eyes began to open.

'We're alive, we're alive!' shouted Zula excitedly. The others very slowly rose up from the floor, propping themselves against the wall of the ship and coughing against the dusty air. The other Evaders also regaining consciousness and coughing as they began to sit up and rouse those who were still unconscious. The five Evader friends all hugged.

'Let's be thankful we are alive,' said Zeno, whose face was white, covered in dust.

It was a relief for all of them that the subtle warm light of the ship had returned, for without this at least, they knew there wouldn't be any hope of survival. There was a crackling sound from the tannoy system and suddenly their sighs of relief and joy were interrupted.

'Are all Evaders all right?' asked the voice over the tannoy system.

'Stupid question!' grumbled Fusion, abruptly shaking his dust-covered features to get the dust off, and brushing down his green shiny trousers.

'We appear to have landed inside a mountain,' continued the message. 'The doors will open for us to explore. Do not touch anything outside.'

Fusion huffed loudly. Electra was shaking as if cold and was looking vulnerable, and Zula placed a reassuring arm around her shoulders.

'We'll be safe now, Electra. You'll see,' said Zula calmly.

'But there are nasty aliens on this planet,' Electra replied, looking back up at Zula. 'They tried to hurt us.'

The Evader friends looked back at each other, reminding themselves of this new and unpredictable situation they were in. What was outside?

Their moment's silence was interrupted by a high-pitched hissing sound coming from one of the wide main doors to the ship. The metallic door rose slowly upwards. All the Evaders in the main, open-plan part of the ship went silent; there was a nervousness and apprehension amongst them. As they started gingerly moving slowly towards the exposed entrance, they could only darkness outside. It was a great unknown, as they ventured further to the edge of the large doorway, turning their heads in all directions, looking forward for something to catch their eye.

'There's nothing out here,' said one of the Evaders, who was bravely hanging halfway out of the ship's entrance to have a good look.

PING! At that moment, three Evader controllers appeared from the circular lift system in the middle of the ship, its door entrance of the ship, in the process, the others moved to one side as if creating a pathway and watched what would happen next. The next three Evaders took one quick look outside the door. They then pressed the large square panel to the right of the entrance and immediately, the walkway appeared from the floor of the ship and descended outside onto the dark ground below.

'This is it!' said Magenta excitedly, rubbing hands together.

'Be quiet!' snapped Fusion. Magenta pulled an ugly face in return. The three Evader controllers walked cautiously down the slanting walkway to the ground, nervously watched by all the others. Was it safe? As they continued their way, their silhouettes disappeared against the blackness as if swallowed up. The others waited anxiously. One minute passed. Two minutes passed. They began whispering amongst themselves, now worried, and then suddenly, the three silhouettes reappeared to the applause and relief of the others, and better still, they returned with their faces looking more relaxed than before.

'Phew,' said Zeno. 'I was worried there for a moment.'

As the three controllers walked back up the long ramp and into the ship, one of them stood on the side of the doors entrance and pressed a large button on the control panel, and began speaking quietly into it.

The Evaders leant forward, eager to hear what was being said. Suddenly, and to their amazement, they could see a warm glow of light coming from the entrance of the doorway and portholes of the ship. They had managed to gain from the ships power supply, enough energy to turn the outside lights on, illuminating their mysterious outside surroundings. Now at least they could explore properly!

The Evaders started whispering amongst themselves, and then cautiously started to wander down the ships walkway to explore.

'You go first,' said Magenta, giving Fusion a hard push forward. Zeno decided to venture outside first and then the others reluctantly followed, slowly making their own way down the slope. The air felt much colder and as they glanced around, they could see that the ship was lying in what appeared to be a giant cave. The space around them was immense. The walls of the cave were illuminated almost in a hue of a very dark red, a rock surface all around them wherever they turned. As they looked high above their heads, they could make out what was the entrance where they had unexpectedly dropped in. They could see the sky high above their heads, a thousand feet up, probably more, and they could just make out the bright sun peering through the top.

'Look at this place! It is huge!' said Zula, amazed. Unbeknown to the Evaders, the ship had by chance landed in the most inconspicuous of places - a caldera, the inside of a huge and long dead volcano. It was for the Evaders (for now anyway) a safe haven, where they could stay hidden away from the hostile alien world outside.

As they waddled further around their new surroundings, now all lit up with a warm hue from the ship's lights, they were able to hear a trickling sound coming from the edge of the cavern. As many of the Evaders began to wander over to the direction of the noise, they could see to their amazement what appeared to be a rock pool with water gently flowing down over the curvature of rocks from high above and glistening amongst the light of the cave. One of the Evaders, unlike the others, decided to venture over to the edge of the rock pool, carefully stepping over the rocks along the edge, and leaned over to taste the trickling water that was flowing down against the rocky walls. Cupping its long hands together, and filling them with water, the Evader hesitated, then slowly tasted the water as the others anxiously looked on. Again, the Evader tried the water, almost placing its whole face into its hands.

'Well? Can we drink it?' asked one anxiously. 'Umm...' replied the Evader licking its mouth with a rather long tongue, almost teasingly.

'Very nice fresh water!' a reply came, which was hopeful and enthusiastic.

'We may live after all!' said a voice loudly.

As the Evaders wandered around their new surroundings, weighing out the realistic chances for their survival, a sudden realisation downed upon them.

'Where are the other three ships?' asked Magenta, who, standing quite prominently on a slightly raised mound of rock, brought the attention from the other Evaders who were milling around and still appearing in a bit of a daze.

Now the Evaders realised their ship was the only one out of the remaining four to have obviously escaped the attack from the alien beings outside. Now all the Evaders turned to each other in frantic discussion, wanting to know the whereabouts of the other Trillion ships.

'Have the aliens shot them down?' Zula asked Zeno but Zeno, like all the others, had no obvious answer.

'Perhaps they flew to safety too,' replied Zeno, trying to be optimistic but realising that perhaps the others hadn't been as lucky as them. The hundred or so assembled Evaders now had to console themselves with the prospect that they were the only survivors from their home planet, and that many more of their friends had gone forever. The Evaders were now once more feeling vulnerable. They had all been through so much, and now had the worry of what lay ahead.

Their thoughtful silence was interrupted by the sudden presence of the six Evader masters, who now descended down the long ramp of the ship and into the subtle lighting now inside the volcano crater. Unlike the others, who were dressed in various colourful array of shiny suits, the masters looked more authorised in their swathes of silver robes, although almost identical in their appearance. Their heads were held high and proud. The six masters stopped when they reached the bottom of the ramp. With long slender hands clasped together, they began to speak, having gained the full attention of the Evaders who apprehensively looked on.

'I have bad news, Evaders. The other ships did not make it. For now, we must try to survive here until we find a place elsewhere to live. We will have the power to explore this alien planet, albeit a hostile one, using the Whizzers to get us around. These will only be used for surveillance purposes and gathering food sources. Any questions please see your Evader team leader.'

Then the message ended, and the six leaders turned around, and majestically wandered back up into the ship, leaving the puzzled Evader population behind.

'What team leader?' asked Magenta. 'We don't have one!'

The others just looked back at Magenta, blankly shrugging their shoulders. Now, with their sense of leadership gone and lost faces all around, it had to be decided amongst them as to who was going to do what. Their priority now was surviving and exploring. At least they had fresh water, which for the Evaders was the most crucial element they needed. The second one was food, and to get that, they had to emerge from the safety of the volcano crater, into the hostile alien world outside.

Chapter 11

So the Evaders went exploring this new planet in search of food in their Whizzers, tiny spaceships the length of the average motor car, but able to fly. These Whizzers were stored at the very bottom of the large Trillion ship, a total of twelve in all, all neatly lined up in a formation of three rows.

A small group of Evaders walked over to the lowest part of the ship, the very bottom of it being embedded slightly in the dark rocky gravel. Pulling a small door panel of the ship to one side, a formation of colourful large controls was revealed, and long agile fingers then slowly pressed the relevant buttons.

A rather loud, echoing noise like a rush of air being released suddenly filled the inside of the massive cavern. From a long ramp maybe twenty feet in length, the ship suddenly descended and gracefully lowered itself to the ground, coming to a stop. The Evaders began to rush forward in excitement, now that the Whizzers were neatly revealed.

'Why couldn't we have started these up and escaped when we were in trouble?' Zula asked, looking at the others, rather puzzled.

'They can't be activated during flight,' replied Zeno. 'The Trillion ship has to be on the ground. But at least now we can go and look for food.'

It was discussed amongst everyone who was going to fly and those selected (including Zeno and friends) ventured up to the sloping ramp and into the base of the ship. As they did this, lights came on automatically, revealing in better detail the circular silver polished mini ships, their smooth surfaces bubble-shaped, albeit only two layers, unlike the multi levels of the large Trillion ship.

Zeno and the others assembled tightly together, now stepping inside one of the Whizzers, its small entrance just large enough for them to squeeze through. Electra got stuck in the process, her large rounded bottom wedged firmly against the edges. With glee, Magenta suddenly rushed forward, and with a raised foot, shoved Electra inside, crashing against the seats.

Now all the Evaders were aboard, they took their positions in the seats that cupped their bottoms comfortably, and they strapped themselves securely in. Zeno touched the screen in front. An assortment of colours projected back, and with another touch of the screen, the Whizzer suddenly came alive with a high-pitched noise, as if woken from a long sleep, and then gently raised itself from the floor like a hovercraft.

Grabbing hold of the sides of the seats with anticipation, the five Evaders turned around to look at the other eleven Whizzers. They too had been started up, and each of the Evaders from the ships waved back at each other, their smiling faces barely showing from their low sitting positions.

With all twelve Whizzers raised from the floor, they began their graceful descent down the ramp, parting the many anxious Evaders who were watching. Now totally out of the bows of the great ship, they began their slow ascent. Up, up they went and as the Evaders watched excitedly through the 360 degrees curved window, all they could see around from the reflection of the Whizzer's lights was rock of very dark glistening red.

As their height increased and they neared the top, the surrounding darkness outside became lighter. Then, to their amazement, the sun and clear blue sky greeted them as they reached the pinnacle of the snow-capped crater. It was a truly beautiful sight. As they gazed outside in awe, they saw the mountainous region all around was white and snow-covered, glistening against the brilliant sun. They hovered for a moment, marvelling at the sight, and then, with a touch of the screen, flew off at great speed.

It had been agreed that all twelve Whizzers would fly in totally opposite directions; the aim was to cover many hundreds of miles radius and explore this new mysterious and hostile world.

So off they flew, Zeno being in charge of the controls. The others sat staring out of the wraparound window, pointing out at anything new they saw as they began to fly away from the mountain region and across desert landscapes. They began to fly over what was the odd small town, and for the first time, the Evaders noticed movement down below, no more than five hundred feet or so, which turned out to be the odd car or truck, and animals running in fields, some in herd-like fashion, which especially intrigued the Evaders. Their main mission was to find food, which for them consisted of vegetation and fruits. But being so distracted by what was going on below was far more interesting.

'Don't get too close,' said Fusion abruptly.

'Horrible aliens!' Magenta laughed.

'No worse than you!' came the reply. Zeno was quietly concentrating on the screen, trying to decide which direction to head in. Electra fell asleep and started snoring, much to the annoyance of the others.

'Electra's off again,' said Magenta.

Zula was transfixed and remained quiet apart from the odd 'Ummm!' and 'Arrhh!'

They didn't want to be spotted by any aliens, so they tried to keep moving, and they only landed twice very briefly, in discreet places hidden amongst trees, for the purpose of gathering leaves and plants. At least they had some food to take back; otherwise they knew they would be in trouble with the others.

After just a couple of hours of flying around, Fusion was starting to get bored and started to irritate Magenta by pulling stupid faces. Then Fusion leaned over and started yanking at Magenta's trouser suit. Magenta responded by pulling back at Fusion's trousers. Fusion then decided to pull one of Magenta's ears. Magenta then stood up and stamped on Fusion's foot. A fight broke out and Magenta and Fusion started wrestling childishly on the floor, in the process waking Electra up and distracting Zula and Zeno from what they were doing. Electra, unusually, decided to join in, then, reluctantly, Zula got involved.

Zeno, meanwhile, struggled to control the side to side swaying of the Whizzer as the others wrestled together on the floor

'Whooohhhh!' Zeno couldn't control the Whizzer any longer, and to the sudden horror of the other Evaders, it began to fall at an angle towards the ground below. The Evaders, who were now all on the floor, rolled to one side, including Zeno, who repeatedly tried to struggle back onto the seat so as to regain the control system but, in the descent, was unable to reach it.

Now there was total panic as they could see they were heading towards the ground, 'ARRRHHH!' they cried out, bracing themselves for the inevitable impact.

'Here we go again!' shouted Magenta loudly.

BANG! The Whizzer crashed landed against the hard surface, landing like a frisbee that had been thrown but not caught. It now skidded along, creating a large display of sparks, the metal of the ship grinding against the concrete surface and making such a terrible screeching noise. The Evaders, their faces now pressed up tightly against the glass, noticed to their horror large stationary objects in their path. And they were heading straight for them.

CRASH! Unbeknown to the Evaders, and to the horror of many terrified spectators, who were running in all directions to escape the carnage, they had landed in the worst place imaginable - in the middle of a supermarket car park. The Whizzer continued to crash into a few more parked cars, smashing its way through with such force that the vehicles rolled over onto their roofs and landed in an unrecognisable heap. To make matters worse, the collection of damaged cars included those of the local police. On hearing the thunderous deafening noise outside, the police ran out of the supermarket, their mouths wide open in disbelief, and promptly dropped their carrier bags containing their lunch.

The scene was one of devastation. A whole diagonal length of parked cars had been literally swept to one side, and had piled up on top of other cars. Smoke filled the car pack and people stood all around, motionless and dazed. Fortunately, most had witnessed the little spacecraft fall from the sky, as its approach had at first appeared to be a large bright light that just happened to get bigger and bigger.

Although the abrupt crash landing was a hard one, they were very lucky. They could have been badly hurt. The Evaders were lying in a heap on top of each other, their faces squashed hard against the window of the ship as it now lay upside down. They did look a dishevelled mess.

'We've landed,' said Zeno calmly.

Magenta and Fusion looked at each other, somewhat embarrassed. It was their fault entirely that the ship had crash-landed.

'Sorry,' said Magenta to Zeno, her ears and face drooping, looking very embarrassed and sorrowful.

'It was your fault,' said Fusion quite madly, trying to pick himself up from the floor but not succeeding.

Zula, whose face now looked a disjointed mess, with all facial features and ears pointing the wrong way, quickly shook her head, shaking everything back into place.

'Behave yourself, Fusion. This is all your fault. It's about time you acted your age,' she said.

Fusion responded by pulling a sarcastic face back at Magenta.

'Is everyone all right?' asked Zeno trying to distract the others.

'How's Electra? Has anyone checked?'

Electra lay fast asleep, curled up in a tiny ball on the floor under a seat, her face still squashed and dishevelled from the impact of the crash.

'Someone wake Electra,' demanded Zeno.

Suddenly, above the sound of Electra's snoring, they could hear a very loud noise of something hovering above them. It was a police helicopter.

As the Evaders looked above their heads towards the noise, they couldn't see anything; instead they heard an announcement coming from the flying machine above:

'DO NOT ATTEMPT TO MOVE, STAY WHERE YOU ARE!' The voice sounded as if it meant it.

Just to add now to the Evaders' sudden fear, they could hear a thunderous roaring echo coming from the ground. The Whizzer began to vibrate. They looked outside the window. Coming towards them was a convoy of dark green military vehicles. As they neared closer, they towered over the collapsed Whizzer. The Evaders peered up in awe as the truck and cars came to an abrupt halt alongside the Whizzer.

As the Evaders peered out, at eye level, they could see the large, menacing-looking tyres of the truck. The front wheels looked threatening as if about to run the Evaders over. As they stared out, they noticed a series of army boots coming towards them, slowly, as if creeping.

'OH NO!' panicked Zeno 'QUICK, HIDE!'

Only problem was, there was nowhere for them to hide. It was such a tiny spaceship. The Evaders could hear human voices, mumbling quietly.

'Let the other Evaders know we are in danger from Tridons,' said Magenta whose face was now frightened and nervous.

'We can't,' whispered Zeno. 'I've already tried. Control panel's broken.'

There was a loud knock on the outside of the Whizzer

'Everyone remain quiet and still,' whispered Zeno. 'They might go away.'

Chapter 12

Zeno, Electra, Zula, Magenta and Fusion were in trouble. There was no escape. Now there were ugly hairy looking faces pressed up against the window of the ship - not a pretty sight, with their hands shielding their eyes, noses and moustaches squashed up, squirming for a better view.

From the outside of the Whizzer, the military were unable to see anything inside. As it was a one-way window, only those inside, could see out. To the Evaders, the faces were almost as ugly as those of the Tridons.

'Let's all remain calm and quiet,' whispered Zeno.

The moment Zeno said this, both Magenta and Fusion started to cry out very loudly indeed, covering their eyes with their own hands as they did so.

'QUIET!' commanded Zeno at the top of his voice in a slow fashion. Zula and Electra, who was now abruptly woken from her peaceful sleep, now struggled to cover their eyes, their faces screwing up.

'BE QUIET!' cried Zula.

Suddenly, they all went alarmingly quiet, as above their heads they could hear a crackling sound coming from outside. The humans were using a powerful blow-torch to try to cut through the metallic roof of the Whizzer. Sparks began to appear above their heads. The Evaders shuffled quickly to one side to avoid the sparks flying in all directions, which were almost landing on them. The shape of a large circle began to form above them.

'They're trying to get us!' cried Zula.

As they nervously watched above their heads, the circle containing the flying sparks was complete. To the horror of the Evaders, something on the outside then tried to kick in the circular form, until they succeeded, and with such a deafening bang that echoed with the Evaders covering their ears, it crashed to the floor of the Whizzer. There was a sudden abrupt ray of sunlight above them, the Evaders immediately flinging themselves to one side of the Whizzer, trying not to be noticed by the aliens now wanting to invade their little private space.

Zeno, Electra, Zula, Magenta and Fusion were frightened. These aliens were louder and bigger than the Evaders, and more intelligent than Tridons. Now they knew they had nowhere to escape to.

Frustratingly, as the Whizzer had crash landed upside down, the Evaders were unable to grab hold of their Glugers that were stored away in one of the holds, underneath the control panel, that was now too high above their heads for them to reach.

Large plastic sheeting was held up all around the top of the Whizzer, concealing everything from the watching world. Suddenly, long arms appeared from nowhere, grappling around with such ferocity, trying to grab an arm or leg. One by one, the Evader friends were lifted abruptly out of the Whizzer, these humans caring nothing for dignity. Their legs dangled helplessly, and their cries were not heard.

'Go into mode two,' whispered Zeno discreetly to the others as they sat together while their little arms were yanked harshly back and handcuffed.

'SAY NOTHING!'

An enormous crowd had gathered at a distance around Best Buys supermarket car park. The military pushed them further away, but the curious crowd just pushed back. There were military and now television helicopters hovering loudly above. 'What a mad hostile world was this?' the Evaders thought to themselves.

59

They were bundled, literally, into the back of a large black vehicle, whose inside was padded white throughout. Fortunately, this made for a soft landing as they fell inside. The door of the van slammed behind them, and now the only light inside came from a small window at the rear of the vehicle, which was too high for them to see through. Unfortunately for them, they were not alone as had hoped. One of these alien beings, large in stature and dressed in dark green military attire, looked the Evaders up and down, as if studying them. The alien sat motionless at the end of the van door as if keeping a safe distance. It just watched, only blinking occasionally or moving its eyes up and down, and it didn't say a word.

'Evaders, are you all right?' whispered Zeno.

Electra, Zula, Magenta and Fusion each nodded. The van wobbled from side to side for a moment, as the aliens jumped into the front of the vehicle, the Evaders fortunately being separated from them by the inside partition and window. The aliens in the front, turned around revealing ugly miserable faces, and they in turn, stared at the Evaders.

'I'll give them something to look at in a moment,' said Fusion under his breath.

The aliens turned back around and then the engine started with a sudden jolt, and then the van started to move off. It was a bumpy ride ahead.

The Evaders wondered where they were going to be taken to and were worried what might happen.

There was no way for them to contact the others back at the old extinct volcano; any last prospect of contact was left back at the Whizzer, which unbeknown to the Evaders had also been confiscated by the aliens.

'What shall we do?' whispered Zula.

'We mustn't worry,' replied Zeno.

The others will soon realise that something must be wrong when they notice our Whizzer hasn't returned.

They should send a search party out for us. But secretly, Zeno knew there was little hope of them being rescued.

Meanwhile, back at the bottom of the old volcano, the Evaders now were having somewhat of a party amongst themselves. They were celebrating their survival, and it was arranged by the Evader leaders for a celebration to be had as a form of keeping their spirits up, as they knew that unhappy Evaders were not constructive ones. The once dark and cold looking surroundings were now filled with a warm orange glow from the fires that had been made, with circular form of rocks in all places, filled with gathered wood. The flames from each one flickered high, as if dancing, matching the merriment of the Evaders dancing around to the sounds of Evader music and song. As it was, the absence of the five Evader friends had not yet been noticed, even though all the other Whizzers had returned safely back from their short exploratory missions.

Meanwhile, the unknown journey began for the Evader friends. The van containing them was escorted by both military and police vehicles, not only in front and behind, but also by police cars on either side. As the convoy continued at a steady 40 mph, both police and television helicopters above dominated the scene. The television film crew in the helicopters were particularly hazardous, as trying for the best possible pictures, ignored the orders from both the military and police to fly at a safer distance. They created an almost constant hazard by such a low level of flying and narrowly missing electrical wires and the occasional petrol station sign in their quest for a better picture. 'GET CLOSER! CLOSER! Hold it steady… steady… WHOOOHHH! It was an alternative ride to a roller coaster. Other helicopters from other TV stations suddenly appeared, adding to the chaos. As they eagerly filmed, the live pictures were beamed across the world, with the headlines that no one would ever expect to hear in real life: 'ALIENS LANDED AND CAPTURED!'

The whole world eagerly watched, bringing a large majority of civilian life to a temporary standstill.

The Evader friends were almost deafened by the noise from the helicopters low above and tannoy announcements going on outside repeatedly saying:

'GET BACK! KEEP YOUR DISTANCE! YOU ARE UNDER ORDERS!'

But all orders from the military and police, from both air and the ground, were ignored. One of the persistent helicopters who had reported from 'FLASH NEWS' had speculated to the world where the convoy was heading for. The young reporter, Katy Wayne, although clipped into the helicopter in a safety harness, hung precariously from the edge of the helicopter side doors that were wide open for the best camera views. The cameraman, also wearing a safety harness, held firmly onto the edge of the door with one hand, camera perched nervously in the other.

'No one knows how many aliens are being transported or where exactly they are going to, but there is strong speculation the convoy is heading for Kantower Mountain, a top secret military installation located just forty miles from here,' reported the eager young journalist to the outside world. This was her biggest news scoop yet.

The journey for the Evaders became increasingly tense as time passed. Not understanding what was making the almost unbearable deafening noise outside and the aliens amongst them constantly staring, watching their every move, made for an uncomfortable ride. The motions of the van became more unsteady as they began to travel over more unmade dirt track roads, and the van at unexpected moments, swung from side to side as it turned around sharp bends, throwing the Evaders off their seats around against the padded interior. Yet still the alien stared…

Chapter 13

The sounds from the roaring helicopters above gradually grew quieter as the van began to slow down and then came to a halt. The alien sitting at the end of the van with the Evaders, suddenly stood up and peered outside the only window, that was placed too high for the Evaders to see through. It was the only movement the unnerving alien guard had made during the entire four-hour journey.

The Evaders looked up at the tall figure, noting any expressions on its face as it continued to peer outside. Suddenly a crackled announcement came over the radio set the alien was holding and it spoke for the first time.

'Roger that.' The Evaders looked on intently.

'I hope Roger is friendly,' whispered Fusion looking at the others. Suddenly, the van started to move again, this time throwing the Evaders to the floor. The distant sounds from the helicopters above became even more silent. They were unable to continue any further; their frustrated filming came to an abrupt end. The world remained curious, wanting to know more. Once again, the van stopped abruptly, this time the Evaders slid along the length of the slippery padded seats. Enormous gates on the outside creaked open. The van started to move once more and this time the Evaders held on firmly bracing themselves for the next time it stopped.

The van travelled a hundred feet, when it stopped again, and this time the Evaders were more prepared as they clung firmly to the seats. The tall alien stood up again receiving a message on the radio.

'Roger that,' it said. And as the van started to move once more, the inside of the padded van grew darker.

The Evaders looked up and all around them, now beginning to feel anxious as the light gradually disappeared.

'Zeno, what is happening?' whispered Zula looking worried.

Zeno clambered up onto the seat and stretched up against the side of the glass-partitioned window that separated them from the aliens up front.

'What can you see Zeno?' asked Magenta.

Zeno now virtually on tiptoes could just about make out the tops of the heads of both the driver of the van and its assistant. As Zeno looked beyond the two heads, out in front appeared a set of huge curved iron doors that must have been some thirty feet high and double that across. Standing either side against the rock surface of the mountain was a number of armed guards. They looked still and menacing, their hands firmly grasping their automatic weapons, with their eyes transfixed on the moving vehicle containing the Evaders.

'Zeno, can you see anything?' repeated Magenta and Zula together, whilst Electra and Fusion tried to clamber up to also get a view from outside.

'Big doors leading to somewhere…' replied Zeno who quickly turned around, and jumped down, and not noticing Fusion and Electra directly behind, knocked them both to the floor together in a heap. Electra had landed on top of Fusion in such a way that none of the others could see Fusion's angry face, as Electra's rather large bottom had fallen unceremoniously on top of it. Fusion's arms and legs frantically began to try to pull off Electra's weight.

Zula and Magenta came to the rescue, grabbing both Electra's arms and legs, and managed to haul her off a very disgruntled Fusion. Before Fusion could start moaning, the van started to move again, this time more slowly.

As it came to another stop after just a few seconds, there was a loud clanging sound that echoed around, as the large iron doors that were now behind them closed. Now the inside of the padded van grew darker, and the Evaders felt the atmosphere becoming tense and almost claustrophobic. The sound of another large set of iron doors loudly creaked open outside.

Once again, the van moved slowly, then after a few more seconds, the van came to an abrupt halt, this time, sending the Evaders falling to one side against the padded seats.

The tall alien stood up, and again spoke into the handset. 'Ready - yes. Roger.'

Zeno looked back at the others.

'Evaders. Whatever happens say nothing!' whispered Zeno.

Suddenly, the rear doors of the van opened, sending an extremely bright flood of light into the back of the van. It was so bright in fact that the alien guard had already reached inside its breast pocket, and conveniently had placed a pair of sunglasses on. The Evaders however, were blinded by the light, and shielded their hands against their faces. One by one, the Evaders were alarmingly grabbed from the back of the van, and with what appeared to be some sort of restraint or lead tied around their clasped hands in front of them, they were then marched down the ramp. The Evaders followed each other one by one and they had a job keeping up with these tall aliens, as their stride was much larger than theirs.

As the Evaders' eyes became more accustomed to the harsh fluorescent lights around them, they could see rows and rows of military personnel lined up, poised as if ready to make the next aggressive move.

The Evaders marched over to a set of doors, each side automatically opening, again guarded with aliens holding weapons, looking menacing with their legs slightly apart. Now their surroundings appeared almost clinical. Clean, bright fluorescent lighting dominated shining brightly, almost reflecting off of the shiny light grey tiled floor and light apple green painted walls.

As they continued their way, with an assortment of smartly uniformed aliens both in front of the Evaders and behind them, towering over, they passed door after door, each one closed. They were mysterious, with no windows, as if holding secrets within. Such endless corridors…

'How much further?' thought each Evader? Not knowing what their fate was now, wearied them even more. What seemed like endless walking, some long five minutes or more, they stopped. One of the officials in front produced a finger and pressed it against the control panel, and the door graced itself open to one side, disappearing into the wall itself. Zula, who was the furthest Evader in front, stood perfectly still, but now shaking as if cold, with head bowed low most subserviently, and now tired.

To the dismay of the other four Evaders, one of the tall aliens took hold of Zula's small shoulders with large but gentle white-gloved hands, as if being coaxed into the strange brightly lit room. Zula silently walked into the room, head still bowed, then as she turned around to look back at the other Evaders with big frightened eyes, the door slid shut as quickly as it had opened. The other Evaders gasped, and their eyes wide and mouths opened with worry.

'Oh no!' They each had the same thought: would they ever see Zula again?

Other immaculate white-gloved hands from those towering behind each Evader were placed gently on their shoulders, as if now they were being coaxed to march on again through the endless bright corridors. Fusion was the next Evader in front. The same thing happened again. A door slid itself open automatically to one side. Fusion turned around looking directly back at Electra, Magenta and Zeno who in turn looked anxiously back. They knew that there could be no communication between them in front of these aliens as the Evaders were secretly hoping that these aliens would be disinterested in them and then just let them go. It was the best if not, only chance they had.

Again, white-gloved hands from behind guided Fusion into the brightly lit room, this time, before the door slid quickly closed, Zeno strained to see what exactly was in the room. To Zeno's shock, he could make out a table of some sort; covered in white sheeting, with what appeared to be tall standing trays on either side. Before Zeno could get any more details of the room, the door slid back closed in a split second. Then a reluctant Fusion was gone.

The walk continued through yet more corridors; Electra now having the smallest stride, was tired of struggling to keep up the pace, and suddenly fell to the floor. The parade suddenly stopped. Zeno and Magenta looked on concerned, although they knew that Electra when tried or bored, as often was, would just collapse anytime, anywhere for a sleep. Marching or not marching. Many white-gloved hands appeared from nowhere very quickly, and carefully picked Electra who was now sleeping curled up on the floor, and was carried into another room, exactly the same as the others. The door slid closed. Now Electra was gone.

Magenta was next in front. As they stopped once more, Magenta was gently coaxed into a brightly lit room, the table draped in white sheeting, clearly exposed; the metallic trays displayed either side. As before, the door slid shut, Magenta turned around to face the official aliens standing intimidatingly close behind. Then the door slid shut. Zeno was last and now alone, and missing being with the others. A huge vulnerability swept over him, almost draining Zeno of any more energy to continue. Zeno's legs now felt very weak as if lacking in any sensation, the realisation of what was happening became too much.

'I will never see my friends again,' thought Zeno, ready to collapse. Before Zeno started to collapse, they stopped for the last time. The door opened. Zeno squinted at the room. Bright lights, table… the room was spinning in all directions… spinning … spinning… and Zeno collapsed on the floor.

Chapter 14

The song and dancing slowly came to an end back at the bottom of the old volcano. The fires began to burn down much smaller, and then the Evaders now more relaxed and merry, began to settle themselves down for a good night's sleep. They certainly needed it after all the emotional ups and downs. Many of the Evaders sat down around the fires, contemplating their future, and what the next day would bring.

'Vino. Go and see if all the Whizzers are secure for the night,' asked the Whizzer watcher, whose job it actually was to check if they were all switched off properly and shut up securely for the night, but was feeling too lazy to do it. Vino gave a big sigh, reluctant to move from the comfortable sitting position against the flickering rock wall. The fire beside it was lovely and warm, the flames smaller but still dancing. Vino slowly got up muttering under its breath, and shuffled over to the colder part of the enormous mile wide rocky space where the Whizzers were now quietly positioned as if asleep.

'One, two, three, four, five, six, seven... eight, nine, ten... eleven... counted Vino from an approaching distance

'That can't be right!' thought Vino.

'One, two, three, four, five, six, seven, eight, nine, ten, eleven... there should be twelve!' shouted Vino loudly. Unsure, Vino counted once more.

'No definitely only eleven!'

Vino in a delayed reaction then panicked, and began shuffling back to the others as quick as its uneven legs could manage.

'Only eleven…huff…huff…only…ELEVEN!'

Vino reached back to the others, in a dishevelled sweaty mess, 'ELEVEN!' shouted Vino at the others, its voice echoing throughout the vast open space.

'It must be later than that!' the reply came.

'No, NO!' replied Vino, breathless. 'There should be twelve Whizzers! One is MISSING!' Suddenly, all ears and heads pricked upwards, alarmed.

'Which one is missing?' asked the Whizzer master

'Number eight, from what I can see,' replied Vino slowly gaining its breath back.

'Who controlled number eight?' asked the Whizzer watcher. An Evader with a high pitch voice now spoke.

'We think it is Zeno!' the reply came. Now there was a hushed discussion. It was decided that a search party would be sent out to find the missing Whizzer, but not until the next return of daylight.

'We will go out and search then,' said the Whizzer leader.

'There is nothing we can do in dark night.' Once again there was hushed discussion, many of the Evaders gathered around, began shrugging their shoulders and shaking their heads. Many hours passed through the night, as the Evaders at the bottom of the quiet volcano, slept.

At first light, the early morning rays from the sun high above the caldera gradually awoke the Evaders from their sleep. But for many it was a restless night, not knowing where their fellow Evader friends had disappeared.

Perhaps they crashed?

The eleven Whizzers were started up; the five members of the Evader crews on each routinely went through the pre-flight checks. Everything was ready and in order.

'Good luck!' cried the other Evaders who began waving at those eager to fly off and find the missing Whizzer. The ships gently rose from the rocky ground, each swaying gently as they did so. As they gathered height, the Evaders below waved enthusiastically until they could no longer see the Evader crews.

As they in turn reached the top of the caldera, the bright sunlight almost blinded them, so it was ordered immediately for the antiglare shields down. It made for an abrupt awakening, now that the Evaders had to become accustomed to a much darker environment below.

As the Whizzers gathered more height, they each glanced below at the beautiful snow covered mountain region that went as far as the horizon as far as they could see. All around was the most beautiful blue sky, cloudless and still.

The mission was on. 'WHOOOSSHHH...!' At an incredible speed, the Whizzers disappeared in all directions, their vision Whizzer trackers at the ready. Whether the missing Evader ship had crashed or not, wherever it was, the Evaders were determined they would find it. But if they didn't, then they would have no choice but to leave them behind as they knew that the Evader population had only a limited time left to stay on this planet. Their mission would be to get the large Evader ship working again so that they could resume their search for a new home. Missing Evaders or not.

Chapter 15

Zeno slowly felt the sensation return to his body, as if waking from a heavy sleep, but his eyes remained closed. The air around felt cold and there was a sense of a presence all around him. Feeling very dazed, Zeno struggled to open his heavy tired eyes lids.

'Oh, such brightness!' thought Zeno, and closed them after what was a split second. Now Zeno could feel the heavy presence of light on his eyelids, it was so strong and blinding, he had no option but to keep them closed. But now Zeno wondered where he was. His body felt as though it was resting on a high surface and not on the floor. The presence above his body felt more intense, almost as though there was something or someone hovering closely above, especially over his face, his eyes now tightly closed against the light. Zeno now felt he was being watched or studied. He remembered now that his Evader friends had been abruptly taken away into separate rooms. A rush of panic took hold of Zeno - the instinct now was to escape!

But no!

As Zeno tried frantically to move as if trying to get up from the hard, cold surface no wonder he felt so cold and bare - they had removed his jumpsuit. Zeno was totally unable to move, as if completely paralysed from head to toe 'I can't move, I can't move…' thought Zeno. The feeling of being pinned down and studied was overpowering. Zeno began to cry out, but as he yelled for help hoping someone would hear, Zeno's mouth was suddenly prized open by two pairs of rubber hands, stretching his mouth so tightly open, it hurt. To the horror of Zeno, another pair of hands from somewhere above him, stretched out what was a long roll of thick surgical tape and instantly placed it over his mouth.

'That should do it,' said a voice. Now he was totally unable to make a sound and his cries could be heard no more. Now no one could come to help. This made Zeno struggle even more, and the helplessness was unbearable.

He began to feel exhausted and physically drained, as his whole energy and emotion was trapped, it was becoming almost suffocating.

Then Zeno could feel someone above beginning to prod his feet all over, the rubber fingers pressing firmly, some movements harder than others, and some even hurting. It was as if Zeno was being examined, and those above were cruelly testing his pain tolerance. Then suddenly sharp stabs of pain gripped his feet to the point of being unbearable. His feet were being stabbed with a needle! The same grappling and stabbing continued, as if being carried out in a sequence.

After the feet, the variations of pain slowly ventured up to his legs and it was here that the pain was worse. As the result of continuous struggling, Zeno's head and body now felt so hot, and was sweating profusely. The sharp prodding and probing around his body stopped. All of a sudden, the blinding light was so strong that Zeno had no choice but to keep his big eyes shut, but the surrounding air now felt thicker and more intense as if something was about to be placed over his face. It suddenly became less bright, which came as a welcome relief. Zeno opened his eyes. 'ARRHHH!' muffled his voice loudly through the surgical tape. Hideous looking aliens, four in total, stared at him so closely above, that their noses could have touched Zeno's face.

'Get me away from here!' muffled Zeno again.

One of the aliens pulled away and spoke, removing a pair of powerful magnifying glasses.

'This is such an interesting specimen. Never thought we would catch one alive and in such healthy condition.' came a voice.

'Unlike the others' said another voice, also pulling away from Zeno.

'One in particular, it's a job to tell whether it's alive or dead!' said the alien, removing its magnifying glasses placed on top of its forehead.

Zeno listened on alarmingly. All four aliens were dressed in brilliant white coats and their hands covered in cream rubber gloves, their magnifying glasses almost dominating their appearance, their eyes looked enormous through the lenses.

'What is the time?' asked one of them.

'Almost seventeen hundred hours. General Storm should be here any moment now!' came a reply

'Who was General Storm?' Zeno wondered.

Suddenly, the automatic door to the room flew open. The four other aliens in the white coats sprung to attention, saluting to those that entered, and they now looked nervous. Zeno tried to turn his head to one side to look, but couldn't and the bright lights again blinded him.

The most prominent looking figure amongst those that entered was an alien with a bald head, very big and broad in build, a shiny complexion, illuminating white teeth and the huge angry eyes. He was wearing a very smart dark green military uniform and cap on his bald head. Most prominent of the features, was the impressive display of medals - an array of colour on his broad chest that was almost protruding outwards along with its stomach.

'General Storm sir!' said one of the white coats, acknowledging his arrival. The response and cold and stern and a look of annoyance came over his face.

'What have you found out?' asked the General abruptly.

'It is in excellent good health sir, and spirited.'

The General then walked over to the examining table where Zeno lay frightened, and looked Zeno up and down, his face almost screwing up as if in disgust. Zeno struggled to keep his eyes open, but slowly getting more used to the bright lights above, continuously blinking his big eyes as Zeno wanted to know what was going on. He could see the bulbous alien figure above him, and on seeing its ugly angry face, further added to Zeno's alarm, and began struggling under the straps once more. General Storm then shook his head in response.

'How come this one is moving and the others are not?' asked the General bluntly.

'ARE THEY DEAD? He bellowed.

A nervous reply came.

'We couldn't comment on the condition of the others sir. They are being examined by team B.

General Storm turned around to face the other five smartly uniformed military figures standing behind him, who were waiting almost subserviently for the next instruction.

'What do we know about those large alien ships we pursued? Have they been found yet?'

The military figures turned toward each other, in the hope that the next person would say something first.

'COME ON! COME ON!' shouted the General 'What do we know?'

There was an anxious pause.

'None of the large alien ships have been found sir. We are still conducting an extensive search.

General Storm appeared dissatisfied and angry with the answer.

'You mean to tell me that we have had an alien invasion that has attacked our planet, and we haven't caught the WRETCHED THINGS?'

'No sir.'

General Storm's sweaty face became distorted once more, and large hands clasped behind his back, began to pace up and down the floor, looking downwards, as if in thought. Then he stopped.

'These aliens are not making a mockery out of me. This is no Roswell!'

'THE WHOLE DAMN WORLD KNOWS ABOUT THIS ONE!'

There was a nervous apprehension in the room.

'Sir. We are using the most sophisticated satellite and radar equipment there is to locate these things. Whether they are hidden on land or in the sea, WE WILL find them!' was the determined response.

'Put it this way,' replied the General. 'For the sake of your career and your family, YOU HAD BETTER'.

Chapter 16

It was decided that the Evader friends would be transported to a top-secret military site that was surrounded by desert and mountains. For miles around, the area would be protected against the increasingly curious public; their hunger for further information on these alien visitors would grow more determined and impatient by the day.

Since the Evaders were transported to the mountainside secret base, an increasing amount of people gathered outside.

Several thousand or more began to gather, many holding placards declaring anything from religious beliefs; to 'The End of the World is Nigh'. But most were protesting about the withhold of information the military and government were keeping. The public were entitled to know who and what had arrived on their planet. It had been a long two days since the huge devastating explosion at Sugar Loaf Mountain in Rio de Janeiro, and the mysterious UFO crash at Best Buys supermarket car park.

The world had a right to know. Such was the pressure that was mounting, especially the continuous news channel updates on TV from the various news stations who had camped outside the mountainside secret base as well as the newspapers who were enjoying record reading sales, further goading manipulation.

The powers that be had hoped that this one, such as the incident at Roswell New Mexico, would quieten down and the public's interest would just dwindle and be an additional subject for UFO enthusiast to discuss at the odd UFO convention.

Alas no. This one would not go away. There was nervousness within the government, so something had to be done. It was time for the public's questions to be met.

It was decided that a news conference would be held directly outside the main entrance to the mountainside military base. An enormous marquee was set up along the grassy verge area to the side entrance of the base. It was the size of a football pitch. It was large enough for a raised platform to be mounted inside at one end, where General Storm and other senior figures that included the pinnacle of government, President Presido.

It was arranged on the chilly misty morning of October 19th, a mass of police guards and secret agents dominated the area both inside and outside the giant marquee. Barriers were carefully put up all around the immediate area, guarded all along by police lines, adamantly holding back the throngs of the thousands of people. A majority of the information hungry public stayed at home or work, eagerly awaiting the live news conference on television. This was to be one of those rare events to go down in history.

Eleven o'clock arrived. The national power grid soured to its highest level. Inside the giant marquee, those with the answers sat rigidly at the long, raised table and platform, their hands either intertwined, or their arms tightly crossed as if creating a psychological barrier. Those with the questions crowded eagerly around and settled amongst themselves for the rows of seats, ignoring the priority booked seat numbers by ripping them off.

If music were played, then it would have made a chaotic game of musical chairs.

Now the world's press had gathered, a mass of phones and cameras at the ready. Then a hushed silence was dictated by a woman wearing a very smart red trouser suit, standing on a podium.

'May I have your attention please, ladies and gentlemen? Silence please. May it be remembered, only one question may be asked from any one news station, and must only be those questions that are listed on the sheet in front of you. Any questions not listed will not be answered.'

At the four wide entrances and on each side of the giant marquee, stood the most intimidating, suited and armed security guards, just to remind those journalists who were not ready to conform to such a manipulative show.

The rather loud sea of hushed whispering stopped as President Presido, General Storm and other military and government members, a panel of eight altogether, were each ceremoniously introduced. As each prominent figure walked in, and then sat themselves down, there were blinding flashes from the hundreds of cameras, adding further to the excitement and anticipation of the occasion which was being filmed live for every news station in the world, such was the curiosity.

The same red suited woman on the front podium then raised her hand high in the air, trying to sum up attention from the now noisy crowd.

'Ladies and gentlemen, PLEASE. One question at a time' she shouted, but the noise inside the marquee was so loud, nobody heard her words.

'Mr President, sir!' The first eager question was raised by a man with bright white hair, his face covered in sweat. 'Have you captured live aliens? Suddenly the chaotic noise hushed up, and you could only hear the flashes from the cameras. President Presido gave a little cough as if clearing his throat.

'It is true to say that a flying saucer had crashed in a supermarket car park in the area of Bousville, on the afternoon of October 16th' said the president. The noise in the marquee again was loudly raised in excitement, until another eager journalist stood up and repeated the same question.

'Have you captured LIVE ALIENS?'

President Presido coughed again, almost in a feeling of awkwardness and turned his head and arm towards General Storm who sat next to him, and who was eager to answer the question himself.

'When we examined the craft, we discovered five small beings inside' said General Storm in a loud, deep authoritative voice, the whites of his eyes and teeth almost fluorescent amongst the blinding camera flashes. The temporary hushed silence became loud again, then quickly quietened down with the next question. Another journalist reluctantly caught the attention of General Storm, a woman who asked the next question with the loudest voice helped by the fact she stood out of the chaotic crowd by wearing a bright yellow and black skirt suit, looking more like a giant wasp.

'WERE THEY ALIVE?' she shouted, although she already had the full attention of all, who were now totally and eagerly silent.

General Storm hesitated. 'Out of the five beings we found, unfortunately four were already dead. The other one was barely alive. It had a faint pulse. By the time both beings were carefully transported to a secure area, unfortunately, the surviving one had died,' he said in a deep voice, trying to look sympathetic. But little did the watching world know, that this carefully orchestrated show had an ulterior motive. Whilst this live news conference was being watched by virtually everyone who could get to a television, the eyes that had been scrutinising the mountainside secret base were now conveniently distracted.

From the very moment of the start of the live worldwide broadcast, it had already been carefully arranged for the Evaders to be moved secretly from their captivity from the military base, and be transported elsewhere. That elsewhere was Area 53, a more secure military base which was mainly all underground.

As an additional distraction, instead of the Evaders being bundled into a typical military vehicle as before, their transportation now was disguised as a different mode of transport. On the outside, the van had its usual blue and yellow livery of Baker's Bread and Buns, with underneath in smaller letters 'Delivered fresh to your door.'

But inside, the usual interior had been totally stripped out, the shelves and everything gone. In its place, it was immaculately padded out in white soft plastic cushioned seats, the same type of interior the Evaders had been transported in as before. A row of padded seats were situated on either side and the windows to the van were again deliberately high at the back of the van and blacked out to stop any prying eyes from seeing anything more than bread and buns. Once again, the Evaders had before them an unknown journey...

Chapter 17

It was pre-arranged that the Baker's Bread and Buns van would be discreetly escorted under military guard to the nearest small airfield, some fifty miles away. They would meet up with a specially chartered aeroplane, equipped inside to safely transport the Evaders to Area 53.

Zeno, Electra and Zula were each ushered out of the padded brightly lit rooms they had been kept in individually. After being kept against their will, scrutinized and probed about, lights and cameras continuously glaring on their tired eyes, they each felt disorientated and confused.

But for whatever they had been through, they were so relieved to see each other once more.

'Electra!' said Zeno excitedly as he was ushered towards Electra who stood slumped against the side of a wall in the bright corridor, surrounded by the tall alien beings who constantly watched over her.

'Electra!' said Zeno excitedly and quickly waddled over to her and gave a big hug.

'Zeno I'm so pleased to see you. I never thought I would see you again.' Electra replied in a quiet and very tired voice.

The few days of captivity had taken its toll on poor Electra, who now looked quite frail, her body again slumping against the wall, and her big eyes drooping low showing exhaustion. 'Don't worry Electra, we are together now,' reassured Zeno.

Along the other end of the long brightly lit space corridor, some hundred feet away, was a happy Zula rushing quickly towards Zeno and Electra, and crying out their names excitedly.

As Zula got closer to them, they could see her face soaked with tears. They hugged one another together, but then large gloved hands from all around immediately separated them.

'Have you seen Fusion and Magenta?' asked Zula anxiously, Electra and Zeno looked at one another,

'No.' Both their replies came together.

'Where are they? What have they done with them?' asked Zula, who now was starting to get angry, looking up at the stern faces of the aliens standing around them. 'What have you done to them?' she cried, slowly and as loud as she could, presuming they had trouble understanding. With no response from the bewildered aliens, Zula then unceremoniously stamped on one of their feet!

'NO, ZULA!' panicked Zeno.

'Be careful with these aliens,' Zeno said to Zula. 'They can't be trusted.'

The three Evader friends were then each abruptly pushed in the same direction down a series of fluorescent-lit corridor until they reached the last set of double doors that opened to reveal a huge open spaced area. In front of them, armed guards formed a corridor towards the rear entrance of the Baker's Bread & Bun van. Zeno, Electra and Zula looked around behind the intimidating aliens, in the hope of seeing Fusion and Magenta, but they were nowhere to be seen. Would they never see their friends again?

'Hurry!' a smartly uniformed official standing by the rear of the van told the aliens walking in front of the Evaders, who struggled to keep up the pace with their smaller strides. They reached the rear of the van, its doors closed. The prominent official standing in front of the doors looked anxious.

'We have no more than ten minutes. He said to another similarly uniformed alien who stood directly in front of the Evaders.

'The news conference has just started'. With that, the official turned his back around and opened the van doors, revealed inside was an alarmed looking Magenta and Fusion, who suddenly looking up from their stooping sitting positions, their legs dangling from the high seats, suddenly jumped down excitedly on seeing their Evader friends.

With no encouragement needed to get into the van, Zeno, Electra and Zula pushed aside the aliens and hurriedly struggled up the small steps. With wails of jubilation and relief; they all gave themselves a big hug, all-collapsing to the floor, to the bewilderment of the staring aliens outside. In their excitement, they failed to notice the armed guard climbing up the steps with a loud thud, and the rear of the van doors closed.

The sound of the engine started up, and with a sudden jolt that threw the Evaders around, it departed. With enormous aircraft hanger sized doors that slid open, the Bakers Bread and Bun van, the driver and his armed accomplice both disguised in blue and yellow bakers breed and buns livery. As the van hurriedly sped off past the numerous military personnel standing around in the secret courtyard that was the rear to the mountainside base, a huge set of gates closed behind the van with a loud clanging sound. In a cloud of dust, the van and the guarded entourage quickly sped off.

The mini convoy was clearly designed for any passing eyes not to suspect anything out of the unusual. The two vans in front, both large in size, displayed the outside livery of 'Flash Electrics' and 'Plunge It Plumbing.'

The two vans behind the vehicle containing the Evaders were cleverly disguised, the only difference was, the highly trained military personnel inside, each member non hesitant to draw out their automatic weapons at their sides, should the secret mission be discovered. In the distance behind them, they could hear the helicopters from the various news stations, hovering over the giant marquee. The news conference by now should have about finished.

At a steady 30mph they drove past the rough rocky mountain slopes. The road became quite narrow and winding in places, it was not for the faint-hearted. Looking over the edge of the road over the barriers, and down into the sloping and steep terrain below, much of which being rocky, had many bushes scattered in places with woods down below all around. The gentle sloping down the mountainside continued. Flying above them a few hundred feet above was a helicopter, which was keeping a constant vigil on the convoy below.

Although there were more military personnel flying above watching their every move at a safe distance, the helicopter was disguised as giving the impression of a more innocent presence. The helicopters which was flying so low clearly advertised 'Happy Heli-Tours' with big smiley face logos on the sides.

Looking up at the helicopter in front from the passenger seat of Baker's Bread and Buns, Corporal Dingle then turned around to Sergeant Porritt, who was driving.

'Why didn't we travel by helicopter, sir?' he asked Sergeant Porritt. For a second, the sergeant looked up at the sky.

'I was told it was too risky in case it collided with one of those crazy news helicopters. They're EVERYWHERE!'

'What, they thought it was safer travelling by van!' he continued looking over the edge of the winding road, trying not to show his nervousness.

'We should reach Marmount Airbase within 90 minutes, at this speed' said the sergeant.

They knew that once they reached the bottom of the mountain and on a level road to the airbase, it would be a straight clear road, and would be able to increase their speed. But for the moment, the journey was slow.

The Evaders, meanwhile, had settled down from their joy at seeing each other again. All five of them sat very closely together, huddled up on the white padded seat that ran the length of the van. The winding road they were travelling on was covered in stones and even small pieces of rock that had fallen down from the steep rock face above.

It didn't make a smooth journey, the motions of the van suddenly jumping about on running over the rough objects. The young armed guard sat silent and motionless at the other end of the van. He wore a powder blue and yellow striped suit with matching cap, and a large company logo of Baker's Bread & Buns displayed on his left breast pocket. His attire appeared innocent enough until you looked at the holster he was wearing, clearly displaying a large gun to his side. Whether this would be used to shoot the Evaders if they tried to escape, or protect the Evaders from an abduction or attack, the Evaders did not know. They didn't want to find out. They kept their distance from the guard, whose face, thankfully, was immersed in a book he had smuggled into the van. The cover ironically entitled Area 53 - The Hidden Truth.

Corporal Dingle almost in a bored daze looked up at the misty grey sky and watching the various helicopters, began to notice something unusual.

'Hey, hey LOOK! That helicopter, it's spinning, it's coming towards us… it's going to crash NO!! Sergeant Porritt, couldn't believe his eyes.

This was not happening! He slammed on the breaks, but with a delayed reaction. Suddenly the van swerved violently to one side trying to avoid the impending impact of the helicopter crashing. Very abruptly, the Evaders in the back were thrown forwards off the padded seats. They collided with the armed guard, whose head banged abruptly against the wall of the padded van, as he had his back to the driver, and being so immersed in his book, failed to brace himself. It didn't help that the Evaders were thrown into him also, with a hard impact, and now they all lay on a mass heap on the floor.

If only seat belt had been fitted for their safety, but for unknown reasons, they weren't.

There was an incredible deafening explosion outside, with Dingle and Porritt and the other drivers in the convoy trying to shield their faces in case of any shattering glass.

What were once the Happy Heli Tours helicopter, experienced a sudden broken rear tail rotor, spiralling it perilously out of control towards the edge of the mountain. As it crashed a couple of hundred feet above them against the mountainside, tumbling into a giant heap of burning wreckage, then crashed in a giant heap of twisted metal and fire directly in front of the Evader's van creating yet another explosion. With panicking cries from Dingle and Porritt, the van swung over to one side to try to avoid colliding with the burning mass. But instead they headed for ravine's edge.

Sergeant Porritt stood on the brakes and his entire face contorted with fear as he desperately tried to stop the skidding van in time. Corporal Dingle continued to panic, and tried to brace himself for going over the edge. Then suddenly, the van stopped. Right on the ravines edge, just one tyres length from going over.

'Phew...' but before they could get their breath back, the two vans that were travelling closely behind them, had no time to react as quickly. 'WHAMM!' with an enormous bang, the Evaders van crashed through the safety barrier sending all three vans tumbling downwards at a steep angle through bushes, narrowly missing the giant rocks, until in a crumpled heap and with smoke already billowing from the crumpled wreckage, they came to a stop in a large cloud of dust.

Chapter 18

As the large dust cloud began to settle, there was now an eerie stillness and silence that surrounded the crumpled wreckages. The only noise around was the lovely sound of the birds singing.

The convoy had finally reached the bottom slopes of the mountainside and in record time but crashing down it was not the intended way.

Each of the drivers and the accompanying military escorts lay slumped motionless. Parts of the crashed helicopter now lay scattered on fire all around, burning out the last of the fuel that had resulted in such a terrible and devastating explosion.

The Baker's Bread & Buns van, no exception for looking a crumpled mess, now lay upside down totally on its roof, part of which had been crushed, such was the violent impact. Both Sergeant Porritt and Corporal Dingle, lay half upside down, part of them still being held by their seatbelts... but looked as if they were trying to do handstands against a wall, but instead just collapsed to one side. Neither one was moving. They looked like they were asleep.

Inside the back of the upturned van lay the Evaders, and the guard. Their bodies all aching and bruised, they lay in an untidy heap on the floor, which now was incidentally the inside of the padded roof. Slowly they began to come around from being so dazed, one by one, disorientated and confused. The padded white interior throughout the van had most definitely saved their lives, including that of the guard, who began to come around, clutching his aching head with his right hand. He was murmuring quietly to himself, not yet fully aware of what had just happened.

The Evader friends began to give each other a good shake.

'Are you awake?' Magenta asked Fusion. Fusion had his big eyes shut.

'I am NOW!' he repeated grumpily as if been he had woken from a sleep.

'Did you HAVE to shake me that hard?' Zeno had a job to shake Zula and Electra awake, as both of them appeared to brunt the most of the impact due to the fact that the others had landed on top of them after all the tumbling had stopped. Zula was the next one to come around.

'Have we landed?' she asked, her eyes looking heavy and weary and was clutching her head with both hands as if she was in pain.

'We have,' replied Zeno.

'Once more we have landed!'

Zula then in a daze, looked over to Electra whom just like her, had been temporarily buried under the others when the tumbling around stopped.

Electra wasn't moving, and was silently lying face down on her tummy.

As the others now looked on worried, they tried to see her making some sort of breathing rhythm, but she didn't appear to be breathing in and out.

'Oh no, oh no!' cried the others now panicking, and all at once, they began to shake Electra hoping for some sort of reaction. Then with a loud snort, Electra's head rose up from the padded white surface, her big eyes still closed tightly shut.

'Arrhhh,' Electra blurted out as if abruptly woken up from a heavy sleep. The others all gave a big sigh of relief. After such a tumble, and being thrown around so much, thankfully, all they had to show for it were sore and aching bodies. The guard appeared to be most injured and bruised, most probably due to his body being much heavier than the Evaders making each tumble harder to bear. It didn't help that the Evaders also landed on top of him.

They anxiously watched the guard; his eyes still closed and still clutching his head and moaning quietly to himself. If was as if the Evaders were waiting for him to notice them.

'Can you see that? Magenta asked the others, and then turning around, to Magenta's amazement, the rear doors of the crumpled van had buckled slightly open and outwards, exposing a gap almost about half way up.

The doors themselves were still intact but in a compressed state. What Magenta felt was that of a breeze coming from the outside.

'Look, look!' cried out Magenta, pointing,

'We can go!' Electra looked back at them with big blinking eyes. 'What if we get into trouble', she replied in an anxious voice.

'Let's go! Let's go!' said Zeno quickly, taking the hands of Electra and Zula. 'Quickly Fusion.' said Zeno.

'The alien is waking up!' Fusion huffed and puffed, and was slow in following the others as they began one by one to push themselves out the buckled doors and then attempt to squeeze through.

'Wait for me…' said a slow Fusion, now beginning to panic as the guard started to wake up from his sub consciousness. But as Fusion was about to squeeze through the gaping hole, the clearance was blocked by Electra who was now so firmly wedged in the buckled gap.

Zeno, Magenta and Zula on the outside of the crumpled wreckage, struggled to pull at Electra's arms, at the same time trying to avoid the jagged pieces of metal that were protruding outwards from the gaping hole. With both hands, Fusion pushed against Electra hard, at the same time glancing backwards at the guard who was slowly trying to get up from the floor.

Then with an extra frantic push from Fusion, Electra crashed onto the stony ground with a thud, landing on top of Zeno, Magenta and Zula.

As they looked up, they noticed Fusion trying to struggle through the hole.

'Don't all rush to help me then!' said Fusion.

Then with no hesitation, Fusion decided to throw himself directly on top of the others, rather than suffering a rather bruising landing on the stony ground.

With grunts and groans, the Evaders one by one picked themselves up from the ground. Surrounding them were pieces of jagged metal, leading up almost into a trail towards the wreckage of the four vans that had before been their military escorts guarding them. This was their chance to escape before the guards came to from their slumber.

'Hey! You there! DON'T MOVE!'

A sudden loud voice came out of nowhere, it was the guard. He had managed to scramble almost half of his slim build through the gaping hole in the van doors, stretching out his arms bracing himself for the impact on the ground. His head was looking upwards towards the Evaders. A look of impatient determination, almost aggressive was etched on his face.

'LET'S GO, LET'S GO!' panicked Zeno, taking Electra and Zula's hands, and running, almost pulling the others along. Magenta was next behind, then Fusion. Normally Fusion could be quite a fast mover as far as Evaders go, but now he began to find himself struggling. In the fall on top of the others, Fusion had a heavy aching pain in his back and ankle, and with each waddle as fast as he could, Fusion could feel the pain even more. The others now were well ahead in front.

'Wait for me,' cried Fusion struggling, and looked around to see the guard had stumbled to his feet and now began to move in a staggered motion towards Fusion, with the guard's arms outstretched and angry.

The guard was adamant on catching Fusion; such was the look of determination on his face showing his gritted teeth.

The space between them closed. Fusion now was limping just a few feet ahead. Fusion turned to see how close the guard now was.

'WAIT FOR ME!' cried out Fusion to the others in desperation. The guard suddenly flung his heavy weight on top of Fusion, and in the struggle, grappled hold of his legs that were now kicking away as he tried desperately to escape. The other Evaders on hearing Fusion's screams, instantly turned around, and all four of them started waddling over to help Fusion as quickly as they could, crying out:

'We are coming, we are coming!' as they did so.

With the guard still grappling frantically at Fusion, the Evaders then jumped on top of the guard, onto his back, his bottom and legs but he did not let go of Fusion. He was adamant that this one was not getting away. Suddenly, out of one of the bushes alongside, was something long and slivery. It was moving. It was coming towards the pile of grappling bodies. The creature was making a loud high-pitched rattling sound, as if it was very agitated.

'Arrhhh! What is this?' cried Magenta and jumped away from the guard at the same time trying to push away Electra, Zeno and Zula.

The long, slithering, rattling creature headed straight for its nearest target, a pair of legs kicking up and down.

With the quickest of movements, the creature flung itself with small open jaws towards the target.

'ARRHHH!' There was a loud yell. The guard instantly let go of Fusion's struggling body, instead, clutching the lower part of his right leg. The guard noticed the rattlesnake sliver away back into the bush where it had come from. The guard rolled up his trouser leg, his face screwed up in pain.

'Oh no, no…' He had been bitten. The Evaders seized their sudden opportunity, and started to run off towards the trees just a hundred metres beyond.

When they reached the wooded area, they all fell to the ground to gain back their breath and composure.

'We had better go back and help the alien.' Zula huffed away to the others. Zeno reassured Zula's concern.

'The alien won't be on its own for long. They will notice we have gone. They will come after us…'

Chapter 19

The Evaders couldn't waste any more time resting. Zeno was right in thinking it would be no time at all until the military noticed the burning wreckages at the bottom of the mountain, and the fact that their priceless missing cargo had not arrived as scheduled at the airbase. It had been, in fact, no more than fifteen crucial minutes between the breakdown in communications in the military control rooms, and sensing that something was wrong.

It was also wrongly presumed at both the mountainside control room and the secret tiny military airbase where the Evaders were heading to, that should an emergency situation arise, contact would be made by the convoy itself.

Had it not have been for the obligatory cup of hot coffee given to the young air traffic controller who had been in constant contact with the helicopter. Knocking the plastic cup containing scalding coffee into his lap caused him to jump out of his seat, accidentally knocking the headphones off. Subsequently, he did not hear the: 'May Day, MAY DAY!' distress call.

For the young recently qualified controller, the timing couldn't have been more ironic, also bringing his career to an abrupt end the moment General Storm discovered, via a rather nervous telephone call from the General's deputy who had just found out the news.

General Storm had just received the unwelcome telephone call just as he and his entourage were leaving the carefully orchestrated news conference.

No sooner had the Evaders been on their top-secret journey to area 53 than they had escaped and gone on the run!

A furious General Storm had a job controlling his immense anger until he and his subservient entourage reached back inside the mountainside base. There was no way he wanted this news to be brought out into the public so soon after the news conference declaring that these aliens were dead. What a national humiliation that would be to the government and the military - and especially to General Storm's pride.

Once inside his black executive car with blacked out and soundproofed windows, the General released his anger like a volcano erupting its explosive pressure. He couldn't hold onto his anger until he got to the base.

'I WANT THOSE ALIENS CAUGHT!' he yelled so loudly that those inside the compressed eight-seater car tried to brace their eardrums against the deafening volume. 'No one makes a mockery of me, ALIENS OR NOT!' he roared.

Chief Advisor Wiseman, sitting opposite him in the rear of the car, lifted his hand subserviently into the air. as if wanting to gain General Storm's attention, but without drawing too much of it to himself.

'Sir. May I suggest. It is going to be rather difficult catching these aliens, perhaps if we did have some help from the public?' he suggested gingerly, almost bracing himself for the answer.

'What?' came the curse reply.

'ARE YOU INSANE? After denying any alien existence in the press conference! What do you think that was, back there?'

Another hand was half raised by the head of publicity for Brainwave Communications, Monsieur Blanc.

'Sir... Wiseman may have an idea. If we get the help from the public, say for a reward leading to capture, we may stand some chance of finding them.

If not, the chances are we won't!' he said with a look of enthusiasm erupting on his face.

'And what about my reputation,' replied General Storm. 'The public will think we've been lying to them.'

All eyes in the car looked on.

'But sir,' replied Wiseman, 'We have been.'

Now there was a silence.

'All right.' replied General Storm reluctantly. 'What do we do?'

'Sir, if I may suggest...' said Monsieur Blanc.

'Yes, yes, get on with it man!'

'If we publicise this and suggest say, a huge reward, say umm... $10 million, for information leading to their capture. Why not get the public to do the work for us?'

You could see the strained look of apprehension on General Storm's face.

It would mean swallowing his pride, and jeopardising all of the top secret information that the military and government had suppressed on their top secret Third Encounter project.

'And tell me, Einstein,' came the sarcastic reply.

'How do we now explain that five captured aliens were dead, but now they have suddenly decided to come alive and escape?' said the General, the whiteness of his eyes glaring back in response.

A reply from Monsieur Blanc emerged quickly. He jumped up slightly in his seat as if the idea had just come into his head.

'We could say that we thought the aliens were dead, but in fact they instead went into a sort of hibernation sleep!' he said excitedly.

'I know,' he continued like an excited child.

'We could issue a special news bulletin later today saying that, during transportation for their burial, which of course was going to be with full military honours...' He paused, then continued, the others all nodding along with him. '...the aliens, unbeknown to us, woke up and must have panicked and escaped!'

'Hummm,' said General Storm, stroking his broad chin and clearly digesting the thought. The others all looked back at the General, anxious for his reply.

'Do you think the public will really buy it?' he said, himself wanting to be convinced.

'Let's put it this way!' said Monsieur Blanc. 'A reward of $10 Million should help to cloud their judgement!

'Umm, yes, yes. We'll have to do it. We have no choice. What shall we hype it up as then?' replied the General back to Monsieur Blanc.

'We could advertise it as something like WANTED - ALIENS ON THE RUN! $10 Million Reward... ' suggested Blanc.

'We can do it' said Monsieur Blanc. 'WANTED - ALIENS ON THE RUN, displaying the $10 million reward! He repeated excitedly of the prospect of arranging a massive campaign and hopefully, he thought, a massive percentage in commission if the Evaders were caught.

'All right then. Let's do it' replied General Storm. He was reluctantly convinced, as he was unable to think of a better solution himself.

The black limousine then gracefully pulled up into the enclosure, within the heavily guarded compound of the military mountainside base.

As the car came to a smooth halt, the doors on either side were automatically opened from those on the outside. Before any of the authoritative figures got out, General Storm had one last thing to say.

'We'll have to make the announcement from my publicity quarters this evening.' His voice was adamant and deep.

'I want you beforehand to go exclusively to the TV stations and tell them we will be re-issuing a live broadcast. I WANT THE WHOLE WORLD TO LISTEN!' he was struggling to contain his anger and frustration, and suddenly grabbed hold of Monsieur Blanc's tie, yanking it harshly to one side.

'This will be the biggest event so far this century. I CONTROL IT! I want those Evaders PREFERABLY ALIVE, IF NOT DEAD!!

Chapter 20

From the moment the Evaders escaped, they hadn't managed to cover as much distance as they would have liked. Their bodies were tired, and they were stiff and aching all over. What probably hadn't helped them was the tumbling down the mountainside. If it hadn't been for the soft padded interior throughout the van, they would most certainly be dead.

The Evaders, whose disappearance had been noticed, had managed to cover no more than a distance of two miles or so from the crash site at the bottom of the mountain. Being so near to the scene itself, they could hear the thunderous noise of helicopters above, and the distant roar of maybe a hundred vehicles descending towards the site.

Since they had not got far, the Evaders had no choice but to take cover temporarily down what could only be described as a large hole within the wooded area. Going almost under the roots of a giant tree, they shuffled together as many leaves and twigs as they could, to try to cover the entrance. Now the light was getting quite dark, darker almost by the minute, they could not only still hear the helicopters in the distance, but more to their alarm, they could begin to see the spotlights too. They were so bright, almost blinding, as the searchlights danced quickly from one side of the wooded area, to another, frantically searching.

'Tawit, tawoo!' a loud eerie sound added further to their fears.

'What was that?' Magenta whispered loudly to the others.

'We are not alone!' he cried, his big eyes wide and frightened. The Evaders huddled tightly together, but only just inside the large hole itself, as each wanted to be able to see through tiny gaps in the broken branches as to what, if anything, could approach them.

'Don't like it here much Zeno,' said Electra.

'I wish we were back with the other Evaders,' said Zula quietly. 'Back on our own planet…'

'Are you all right, Fusion? Zeno whispered.

A grumpy looking face peered up from a crouching position.

'Oh, I am so happy'. Fusion replied, and Magenta and Zula chuckled quietly to themselves.

'Sshh,' whispered Zeno, now barely audible, and with a long finger, pointing to the direction outside.

They could hear the branches of the trees on the ground crunching away under heavy boots, and the sound was getting uncomfortably louder. They could hear the loud voices of soldiers; the Evaders were frantically being searched, or so it sounded like. The crunching sound grew louder, and louder.

As the Evaders peered out so cautiously through their secret little hideout, to their horror, they could see a large pair of black glistening boots and alongside the pair of dark green camouflaged trousers, what appeared to be the butt of an immaculately polished rifle. Zeno quickly placed his hands over Electra's and Magenta's mouths, as either one of them was about to say something to give their position away. The barrel of the soldiers' rifle was thankfully pointed upwards, the butt of it now resting on the leafy ground. Breaking all military rules, and having a good look around him to see if any others were near, he lit up a cigarette.

'Arrhh,' sighed the soldier, savouring a couple of long drawn out puffs. Suddenly soldiers began to appear from nowhere, the crunching sound from under their boots grew louder. The smoking soldier panicked, and quickly squashed the end of the lit cigarette between his thick hard fingers, and promptly dropped it onto the leaves below right in front of the Evaders faces. The soldier quickly moved away hoping that none of his colleagues noticed his quick drag.

The Evaders gave a big sigh of relief.

In the darkness, the others could see Fusion screw up his face more than normal.

'What is that smell?' he asked.

'Oh no! Look!' cried out Zula. The careless soldier had dropped his cigarette onto the dry leaves and now there was smoke waving up into the air. A tiny fire had emerged, the flames beginning to crackle.

'Quickly, quickly'! Zula said to the others. They recognised the small fire instantly and knew how quickly it could spread.

They risked being seen by the dozens of soldiers who were still no more than a hundred feet away, each grabbed hold of a pile of leaves in front of them, and almost at the same time, threw themselves into the smouldering fire. For a moment, they lay there and looked up, were they seen? Were they heard? They kept perfectly still.

The crackling sound under the soldier's heavy boots became quieter until no longer could they be heard. The search lights above from the helicopters continued, the aluminous white light still dancing from side to side, almost erratically, until that too, disappeared into the distance. It seems as though this time they were lucky. The Evaders raised their heads from the ground.

'What will they do if they find us, Zeno?' asked Electra, his big eyes still frightened, and his little body shaking.

'Let's hope they don't,' Zeno replied, stroking Electra's head.

'Evaders. We will stay here until sunlight. It will be safer for us to go on' said Zeno who in a gesture, slowly climbed back, into the large hole in the side of the tree. The others followed. It was a cold night ahead. Although the Evaders were skilled in making a fire to help keep them warm, tonight, right now it was too risky for them to draw any attention to their whereabouts.

Once more they covered the entrance of the hole with the branches and with the dry leaves and moss inside, they huddled together in their attempt to keep warm.

Chapter 21

Finally daylight arrived and it gave them a welcome relief as one by one they woke up. It was going to be a release for them to escape their temporary hideout, and the sunlight peered downwards and through the trees as if goading the Evaders to move on. The birds were singing all around, it was a beautiful, peaceful sound.

Zeno in particular hoped it would be safe now to move on. The area being so close to the crash site would have been one of the first to be searched. It would be unlikely they would come back to search over again.

The Evaders slowly made their way out of the enclosed woods. The trees grew more sparsely around until sunlight once more greeted them with a warmer glow on their bodies. It was good to be out of the dark woods. As they stopped for a moment to look around, and trying to study what was around them, was a road, no more than a hundred metres in front. Not knowing exactly where they were going or what their intentions were, the Evaders began to waddle towards the road. Fortunately for them, there seemed to be no passing traffic to hide from. It was so quiet. Dodging in between the bushes scattered all around, they reached the edge of the road, which consequently in the wrong direction would lead slowly back up to the mountain. It was the only road for miles around, so quiet and used by only that of the passing military going backwards and forwards, and that of the occasional farmer or land worker.

Suddenly the Evaders ducked their heads down low. The noise of a large truck could be heard further along the road and was coming quickly towards them.

'Hide!' said Zeno alarmingly. All the Evaders attempted to camouflage themselves by jumping behind a bush. The bush though, was scarce of leaves, and the bright colours from their tunics and trousers were very obvious to be seen. The truck containing some thirty pigs, roared past, the thunderous noise stopped as the giant tyres came to an abrupt halt just a few short yards from the alarmed Evaders. They were now bracing themselves to be seen.

'Do not move. They may see us,' whispered Zeno to the others. 'Keep very still.'

The driver of the truck on the nearside to the Evaders opened the truck door and with broad back to the Evaders, climbed down the steps onto the side of the road.

The very large driver, his back still towards the Evaders then started to undo the zip on his baggy dirty jeans. Then rocking backwards and forwards on his heels and his head looking upwards, 'arrrhhh,' the man made a loud sigh of relief. He must have been desperate, and a good fifteen seconds later, he redid his zip up, and with a clumsy waddle, wandered back to the truck, this time directly facing the Evaders who were crouching behind the naked bush. The driver whistled away, totally oblivious to the colourful aliens in front of him, but appeared to be looking directly at them.

'The alien can see us,' whispered Zula alarmingly. And the Evaders crouched even lower still, trying not to be seen. Fortunately, the driver opened the door to the truck and took his place back inside. Much to the surprise of the Evaders who had expected the truck to drive off, looked on as the driver decided to reach for his pair of spectacles on the dashboard, and then decided to start rolling up a cigarette.

'Why isn't the alien going? Magenta wondered.

'Shoo! Shoo!' said Magenta then waving her long arms around.

'I have thought of a faster way for us to travel,' whispered Zeno suddenly. 'Follow me!'

Reluctantly, the other four Evaders followed him, still crouching as low as they possibly could towards the truck that was just several feet in front. The driver now wearing his glasses, was too emerged in perfecting his roll up cigarette rather than look into his rear view mirror and notice any aliens approaching.

Zeno thought it a good opportunity, being the resourceful one, to smuggle themselves onto the truck. In whichever direction it was heading for, at least it would help them to think they were moving rather than being somewhere so remote and without the transportation of a spaceship. The truck would have to do.

As they reached the edge of the towering truck, the Evaders looked in front and behind at the massive tyres it was quite a daunting sight. They crept over to the rear of the truck, and now being so close, could hear the snorting loud noises the pigs were continuously making. Randomly the pigs shoved their snouts out between the wide wooden slats, the gaps being some six inches wide, alarming the Evaders, making them jump away quickly. Never before had they met pigs.

Their aim now, was to somehow try and climb aboard the truck, and without being noticed by the driver in front. Zeno cautiously peeped around towards the front of the driver's cab. The large and long wing mirror on the side, revealed to Zeno that the driver was still preoccupied in rolling up his cigarette, and for whatever reason, appeared to be taking his time doing it. Zeno turned to face the others.

'We must be quick. It will go at any moment.' Their eyes glancing around at the back of the truck doors, they noticed that there appeared to be a wooden tiny ledge running along the width of thick wooden planking that surrounded the enclosed pigs.

It was probably no more than 2cm wide, but the ledge was wide enough for the Evaders to slowly climb up. With carefully placed footing, and with Zeno going first, they aimed to climb inside the wide gap between the thick wooden slating containing the pigs. It worked to their advantage having such agile feet and aided by their black rubber skin tight boots, gave them that extra grip they needed.

From the ground itself up to the wide gap they were aiming for, it was only a mere five feet.

Grabbing hold of the edge of the wooded enclosure and with the pigs snorting even louder and beginning to squeal the Evaders one by one squeezed themselves into the rather narrow gap. Zeno was the first one to collapse onto the damp straw below, making a soft landing. With wide eyes and feeling somewhat alarmed, Zeno stared back through the dim light and noticed the pigs squealing loudly in a panic, their space having being invaded by aliens. With the look of panic on the pig's faces, and clambering tightly together in a corner of the truck, the other Evaders one by one, tightly squeezed through the gap, collapsing onto the damp smelly straw. That was, all but Electra, the last one who was desperately trying to squeeze through.

'Pull, pull!' cried Zeno to Magenta, the pair of them taking a firm hold on Electra's arm and leg, and trying to pull him through. But he was stuck!

'What's all that commotion?' thought the driver who by now had just finished rolling his cigarette. He stretched over the dashboard, and reached for his small silver gun. He glanced up into the large wing mirror beside him. With a flick of the trigger, he lit his cigarette.

'Bloomin' pigs, bloomin' noisy things,' and with that the driver reluctantly opened the cab door and heavily jumped down onto the ground. With the cigarette hanging out of his mouth and muttering under his breath,

he waddled towards the back of the truck, pulling up his baggy jeans as he did so, they were almost falling down revealing the top of his grey boxer shorts.

'Pull, pull...' Due to the strain, Zeno's voice was barely audible over the snorting sounds from the pigs.

Zula noticed sudden movement coming from the outside of the truck, its movement casting a dark shadow against the stream of light on the straw below. She let out a loud gasp, and rushed over to grab part of Electra's yellow tunic and quickly gave such a yank. Her panic was evident.

'Arrhhh!' moaned Electra as she collapsed on the straw below.

The driver on reaching the back of the truck, took a good look around him, then with both hairy hands grasping the edge of the wooden slats, peered through to look at the pigs.

'You pig's settle down now. Don't want any more trouble from you!' With that he turned away and muttering under his breath, headed back into the driver's cab, the cigarette now burning much smaller. As the driver jumped heavily back onto his seat, the long, burnt remnants that had gathered at the end of the cigarette, dropped onto his lap. Noticing, he attempted to brush it off with one hand, the other starting up the engine to move off.

With a loud shaking movement, the truck started up, bellowing lots of black smoke behind it. The Evaders now half submerged under a group of pigs, felt some relief that now they were starting their journey, in the hope of getting back to the old volcano and the other Evaders. They didn't quite know how, but at least it was a start.

The light now inside the back of the truck gradually grew darker, as night-time slowly approached. The Evaders now tried, huddled up as best they could in one corner to the rear of the truck. Their heads tried to remain as close to the gaps exposing the outside world, in the attempt to get some fresh air.

Inside the stench was becoming quite overpowering, the straw below them becoming even made damper, although the pigs didn't seem to mind.

The Evaders each looked upwards at the night sky, and marvelled at the beautiful sea of stars above.

Forever it looked so peaceful.

'I wish for home.' Said Zula to the others, and they all continued to gaze upwards, the passing mass of trees either side of the road creating a blur as they sped by. Their eyes now became tired and heavy. There was no other option but to fall asleep. It had been a long and tiring day. What tomorrow would bring, they didn't know. Whether they were heading in the right direction, they didn't know. For now, just sleep. Go to sleep.

Chapter 22

Their night's sleep had passed by quickly. The early morning sunlight had begun to peer through the wooden slats, creating a warm orange glow on the straw below.

As the Evaders slowly awoke, their heads felt heavy and aching most probably not helped by the pigs constantly scrambling from side to side and motions of the truck vibrating heavily against the rough road terrain below, during the night. As their eyes became more accustomed to the daylight, they noticed now at least, that the rough movements of the truck had stopped, as well as the loud sound from the engine. Gradually lifting their tired heads from the smelly damp straw, the Evaders one by one except Electra, peered outside to their new surroundings.

The engine noise began to sound a lower deeper tone, as if it was beginning to slow down. Zeno turned his head to the others who were also hanging onto the wooden slats, peering outwards.

'If we are going to stop, I don't know where.' As the truck slowed down it turned off the road and gradually swerved into a big circle, preparing to park itself alongside a line of other vehicles, an assortment of two scruffy trucks and a few cars. It found its space. The engine stopped. An enormous barn dominated the area, as they pulled up alongside it and just a few yards to one side was a bungalow. They had arrived at a farm. All that could be heard now was the snorting sounds from the pigs. 'Wake up Electra! Wake up!' Zula began shaking her, now feeling a sense of urgency. The driver jumped down from the cab and in a heavy and tired swagger, reached the rear of the doors.

The pigs now sensed that it was feeding time, and began rushing towards the doors, almost in a fast frenzy. Before the Evaders could try to conceal themselves to the rear and cover themselves with straw, the truck door swung open. Immediately, a ramp had appeared from nowhere, landing with a thud on the dusty ground. This was the best excitement the pigs had had in the last eighteen hours, and now sensing their freedom, made a frantic rush toward the new occupants. A huge set of doors to the barn were pulled aside, ready... and before the Evaders even had a chance to cry out in panic or react, they were carried out with the rush. They were swept along out of the truck, and tumbled one by one painfully on the ground, trying to shield themselves from the mass of thundering hooves. The driver on seeing at first, a blaze of bright colours in amongst the flying pigs, and then to notice something else more sinister; strange curled up beings of some sort, made him stare, the cigarette dropping from his mouth.

'These are not pigs.' He said out alarmed.

Not realising the pigs were starting to run in either direction to the side of the truck and not straight into the barn, all that was left now amongst a cloud of dust, were the Evaders. They were curled up into large balls almost at the driver's feet, in what was their poor attempt to protect themselves from the thundering hooves.

'WHAT... IS... THIS!' he bellowed almost breathless. Zeno and the others, their heads now popping up from under their bodies, looked up alarmingly at the big hairy driver whose face looked more alarmed than the Evaders. Without any further hesitation, Zeno firstly, sprung into life and began to waddle off as quickly as his little legs could take him. Almost at the same time, the others jumped to their feet and began to follow Zeno who turned around, waving at the others to hurry.

'Run! Run!'

The shocked driver couldn't believe what he was seeing, and in a delayed reaction, began his pursuit, totally ignoring the pigs that had now all escaped.

Zeno was breathless and encouraged the others to catch up. 'Keep going!'

But although they were running as fast as they could go, the gap between them and the irate driver was closing fast.

Zula, Magenta and Electra were running fast but Fusion was furthest behind and limping. Fusion had hurt his ankle whilst tumbling down the ramp.

The thunderous heavy feet of the driver could almost be felt by Fusion, like an eerie vibration. The driver was panting, breathless as he spoke.

'I'll get you, you rotters!' he huffed loudly.

The gap had closed. The towering bulk took a chance, and literally threw his heavy weight and huge stomach onto the ground in a cloud of dust, in the process, grabbing hold of Fusion's struggling legs.

'Gotcha!' he huffed loudly and began to grapple at Fusion's body in the attempt of keeping him on the ground.

'Awwww!' cried Fusion as loud as his lungs would allow. He looked up, and noticed the others had begun to rush towards him in a panic.

'Let go of me.!' cried out Fusion, his face turning redder with frustration and anger as he tried to struggle free.

Then much to Fusion's relief, the others reached the fracas on the ground and started to pull at his arms.

He felt as though his little body was being pulled in two, further adding to his pain and torment.

Then before the Evaders could do anything else, the strong, bulky driver staggered to his feet, still firmly clutching Fusion.

Now the driver had better height and weight advantage, these small aliens were not going to defeat him, no way. With one heavy swoop, the driver's big hairy arms gripped hold of Fusion's middle, and unceremoniously, slung him over his shoulder, now hanging him upside down with his little legs kicking away.

'YOU ROTTERS!' he yelled kicking away even harder, only for the determined driver to take hold of both his legs, with one broad hairy arm, and hold them down onto his chest.

Fusion's arms were waving around frantically at the others who were just trailing behind the wide steps of the driver.

'Help me Evaders.!'

Zula in such frustration started tugging downwards at the driver's baggy jeans, in the attempt to slow the man down. Magenta and Zeno decide to rugby tackle the driver's legs. Now the big man's steps were coming to a halt, and the driver attempted to shake each Evader off.

'You get off me! You rotters!' he bellowed.

'I'll call the police.!'

But still they clung on. Then an unexpected thing happened. The driver's jeans could take no more and with a broken belt, they fell down with one quick swoop.

'You rotter's! What have you done!' he shouted.

Revealed was the most awful pair of boxers, so big and baggy. They were probably white originally, but after so many washes, the colour now a disappointing murky grey. The buttons on his shirt, now pulled open, revealed a large hairy tummy, hanging over the grey boxers. Such was the panic, the public humiliation, in front of such strangers, was too much for the driver to bear.

His pride diminished, and looking downwards, he accidentally lost his firm grip on Fusion, throwing him heavily to the dusty ground below.

'Ouch!' cried Fusion, further adding to his humiliation.

'Run, quickly run!' said Zeno 'WE GO!'

With that and holding onto each other, almost dragging along in a line, they rushed off as fast as they could.

As the driver, now enraged, tried to follow, he fails to notice his dirty jeans crumpled low around his ankles, causing him to fall heavily on the ground, in the process, hurting his ankle.

'You just wait! He shouted after them. His face contorted 'YOU WON'T BE ON THE RUN FOR LONG!'

Chapter 23

It had been a lucky escape. As they hurried off as fast as their legs could take them, they frantically looked around in all directions for somewhere to hide. However, the immediate area was barren. Just a series of large yellow fields, but in the distance they could make out buildings. On the horizon was the small town of Bidunott, population no more than four hundred, although growing fast, especially since they had built the first major supermarket on the edge of town.

'I can't go on any longer. I need to rest, Zeno,' said Fusion, the strain beginning to show on his dirty face.

'Not much longer,' Zeno's eyes were focused on the small town beyond. Just ahead of them was a row of trees, and some bushes.

'We will head for those trees and we will rest.' Zeno reassured the others.

'What shall we do after that?' Zula asked.

'We will go over there,' he replied pointing.

'We will find some food and we will find a way of getting back to the others. They should be looking for us by now.' Zeno realised there was probably very little hope seeing their friends again, but knew that if they continued moving, albeit in an unknown direction, they would stand a better chance. Zeno forever the leader, the optimist, and the confident one. The others were looking to him for support. Their nightmare would end, wouldn't it?

'You took your time, back there,' grumbled Fusion.

Interrupting Zeno's thoughts, Zeno and Magenta scowled back.

'We will leave you next time.' Some two hundred metres ahead, and they finally reached the row of trees, their branches mostly bare, but now forming a thick cushioning layer below.

Collapsing to the ground to gather back their breath, they began to look towards the small town ahead of them. Just ten minutes away, they should be there.

Magenta looked up at the clear light blue morning sky. It was going to be a truly beautiful autumn day.

'I can't see any of the others yet,' she said

'Hope they come and find us, perhaps we should light a fire?' asked Electra.

'They will come along, and we will be saved by them. We will then go home…' Oh, such wishful thoughts. If only it could be that easy.

'Yes Electra, let's make a fire and we can all go home and live happily ever more.'

Fusion was in no mood for such whimsical talk, but Electra gave an innocent little smile back, totally unaware of the sarcasm.

'It may be safer for us to venture towards where aliens live when it is dark. We will have to be careful not to be noticed any more,' Zeno said in a more serious tone than normal.

'We will rest here for now whilst it is safe. It will be dark when we wake up. Then we will venture still'

It seemed an easy option for now. They could get some more rest, discreetly hidden amongst the few trees and amongst the long grass and listen to the early morning bird song.

No sooner had it seemed they had rested, when slowly one by one they woke, the birds no longer singing and their heads now feeling heavy.

The warm sunlight for the time of year had long disappeared, replaced by the beginnings of darkness that was quickly to creep over them. It must have been a heavy sleep. Both mentally and physically, the Evaders were being tested to the limits, not realising the toll it must have been putting on their small bodies.

Their arms and legs stretched out, ready to face the night ahead.

'We must have needed such rest.' Zeno yawned, stretching out both arms towards the night's sky.

'Are you all awake, ready?'

Zeno noticed four reluctant heads yawning and slowly nodding.

'Off we go now. Keep close together…'

There was more of a reluctance to move from the comfortable indentations made in the deep cushioning of leaves, now moving to say goodbye to their temporary hideout, further risking being seen once more. How much longer, they thought would this go on? Surely the other Evaders will find them at any moment?

Ahead of them, now lay a recently ploughed field.

Under the moonlight, they could just make out the immaculate wide lines, leading almost directly up to the edge of the town just a few hundred metres away.

As they reached nearer still, all was quiet out from the field they came, and clambered through the wooden fence on the end of their trail. Their feet now landed on concrete, a hard surface. As they looked anxiously around, there appeared to be at first farm buildings, but beyond that as they cautiously waddled through, they came to a quiet road. Directly on the other side of the road in front of them, they noticed a petrol station, small and quiet. There were no customers, no cars, only the station attendant, whose head was buried in a magazine, in a world of his own, picking at his nose at the same time.

The Evaders hoped it was a good magazine, as they cautiously crept by, attempting to hide behind the odd petrol pump and behind them as well as if in front, there gradually appeared to be more and more buildings on either side of the road. The odd car was parked up, silent and with the first signs of frost on windows. Fortunately, it must have been a late hour for everything to be so quiet, much to their advantage.

The Evaders passed a series of small shops, all closed up for the night. As they peered in, they noticed chequered cloths placed over open display areas in the cake shop. The small grocery store next door had shutters at the windows pulled down, not really offering that much of a deterrent, should someone be determined to break in and steal the contents of food inside. Next to that, they wandered past a small restaurant running directly alongside it, was a dark alleyway. Unaware of dangers that could be lurking, the Evaders casually began to wander down the dark alley, leaving the reassurance of the lit quiet street behind them. It was only as far as the rear of the restaurant that they stopped, although they could have wandered further still into the darkness beyond. Along the side of the restaurant by a tall wooded gate, was a collection of dustbins full to the brim with rubbish and thrown out food. It was rather smelly.

To the side of them along a wall, casually piled up, were some cardboard boxes of various sizes, all empty and used.

'Evaders I have an idea.' said Zeno gaining the attention of the others and started grabbing at the boxes, studying them at all angles.

'We can cover ourselves up so that no aliens will be able to notice us. Then we will be able to move around more freely.'

The others smiled and looked at each other approvingly. 'Good idea. I like it and it will certainly improve Fusion's looks anyway!' replied Magenta.

Fusion took offence and pushed Magenta into the pile of boxes behind.

'We could try it, anyway,' suggested Zeno taking hold of some of the larger boxes, and promptly shoved the box onto Magenta's head as she lay collapsed on the ground.

'I can't see anything now!' she moaned, and began punching at the box from the inside, promptly making a couple of small holes in the process.

'Oh, that's better. I can see your ugly face now...'

'That's it. Well done Fusion.' Zeno was further encouraged. The Evaders gathered up for more of the biggest boxes, and placing one on top of their heads, punching away holes, which on the outside, looked simply as innocent wear and tear. From the outside, anyone looking at the Evaders, now would only see cardboard boxes, their legs and small bodies submerged totally.

It was a great idea. Their disguise would enable them to move around, although somewhat awkwardly. No one would suspect anything, otherwise would they?

Their new sense of freedom lifted their spirits. They were about to put their disguises to the test.

'Off we go, Evaders. Keep together now,' said Zeno and with over proportioned feet and slender little legs peering out from below the box, made his way out of the alley, and the four other walking boxes followed. From the punched out ragged holes, they were able to see only directly what was in front of them, anything behind or to the side, they would have to turn completely around.

The street was still quiet and dimly lit. It was four o'clock in the morning. The boxes followed each other, in a line, each one moving in an exaggerated fashion from side to side with each awkward waddle movement they made. Then Zeno stopped. The others not being too aware and still getting used to their restricted vision, collided with the box in front.

'Mind where you are going!' moaned Fusion turning his box completely around to complain to a surprised Electra who had fallen to the ground and landed on her side, exposing the open side of the box with her legs kicking away, trying to get up from the ground.

Zeno had an idea.

'Evaders, I have thought of a better plan.'

With that Zeno took hold of two of the carrier bags and one in each hand, began to drag them along back towards the alleyway. The others looked on bemused, wondering what he was up to. The others began to follow on, each box moving erratically from one side to another as they waddled. Zeno continued dragging the bags along the pavement, now becoming unaware that the bags had started to rip, resulting in a trail of clothes behind Zeno's steps. One by one, the Evaders stopped to pick up each item, stooping down under the box then moving on.

'Zeno you're making a mess!' moaned Fusion loudly as he squatted down one more time to pick up another item of clothing.

'Zeno, these are not ours to take!' Zula was feeling awkward over this.

Zeno stopped and turned around, 'If we look more like the aliens, we will be able to move around unnoticed. We can return to the Trillion ship sooner! Zeno was trying to be encouraging although knew the odds were against them.

So off they trotted back to the alleyway. As they looked through the clothing items, a little more optimism crept over them.

'Perhaps this is not such a bad thought!' said Zula.

There were crumpled up hats, cardigans, shorts, and a very large brassiere, a pair of dusky pink long johns. In the other bag, were an assortment of boots and clumpy shoes.

With all the items thrown together in a pile, the Evaders had a sense of fun for a moment, sorting out who was going to wear what.

There was also an imminent sense of freedom approaching as they began to dress up.

'We will look like the aliens!' said Magenta excitedly, trying on a white fluffy mohair cardigan with huge gold buttons it looked more like a dress, and complemented by a pair of clumpy big brown boots.

'They will not know at all it is us! What do you think, Electra.? Electra…?

The Evaders looked around.

'So where was Electra? She was gone.

Chapter 24

Electra lay fast asleep in her cardboard box, totally unaware that she was missing from the others. Electra had originally made the attempt of getting up from the ground after Fusion had wrongly pushed her over but although she had sat back in an upright position, still gave her the green light to fall asleep.

After all, the others were talking away amongst themselves as they often did, so what else was there to do?

Usually, Electra could fall asleep anywhere at any time within just a minute or two. It didn't take long...

It was now almost five o'clock in the morning. The day was starting to come alive very slowly. The birds were in the throes of singing, ready to wake the world up, all except Electra, anyway. A couple of young foxes appeared just outside Electra's box. They had a good sniff and began to prod it with their noses. Was there something inside perhaps? Electra made a movement in her sleep, moving the box, instantly frightening the foxes away.

Electra was starting to have a bad dream. She was dreaming that The Evaders, in their frantic escape, were running as fast as they could, however the terrifying aliens were fast catching up with them, so big and fierce. So much anger on their evil faces...

Suddenly, all the Evaders are tripped up by something. It was a trap. They fell to the ground. The black shadows of the aliens hung over them...

Electra awoke with a start now looking around, where are the others? Where are they? They are gone. They've left me. OH NO! I'M ON MY OWN.!

A sense of vulnerability swept over her, this time more than ever.

'I must find them...'

Finally arising up from her curled up position inside the box, she got up and started slowly to wander off in the wrong direction and totally unbeknown, began to distance herself further away from the others.

'They can't be very far. Perhaps they are down here?' she thought and made an about-turn down an alleyway.

Electra came to an abrupt halt. In front of her, was an enormous mound of rubbish the dustbins underneath were almost buried.

'I will wait here for the others to return.' With that Electra once more curled up inside the box just beside the street lamp that dimly lit the alleyway that was strewn with rubbish.

The Evaders meanwhile were ready for their rescue mission. Now dressed in their new attire, they could clearly pass as aliens. They were now ready for their mission. Cardboard boxes tossed to the side, they stood in a small line up with Zeno doing the inspection. 'Right Evaders. This is it. Whatever it takes, we find Electra.' For once there was seriousness in his voice and his large bright blue eyes looked more emotional than usual.

'Ah, yes we do,' replied Fusion, his head downwards, nodding. A feeling of guilt had come over him.

'If you hadn't pushed him over...' Magenta was agitated and the look was evident on her face.

'Nothing will happen to him. We will find him,' said a confident Zeno.

'What if we don't find Electra and she is left to the mercy of the aliens?' Zula asked. 'If anything were to happen to her...'

The night's sky now gradually began to turn lighter as they began to wander around in search of their friend. In clumpy high heels, and clothes so baggy and drooping around their small bodies, the first place they headed to was outside the charity shop. Expecting to see a box with Electra curled up inside, they were, to say the least disappointed.

'Cannot be far. Look around Evaders.' Time was passing and they looked everywhere but the right place. They upturned boxes hoping for a pleasant surprise, but nothing. Slowly the town was beginning to spring to life.

It was going to be an extra worrying time for the Evaders. They hoped no one would recognise them. It was now almost seven o'clock in the morning. The aliens started appearing, driving past in the occasional car. Some were turning up at the shops, raising the shutters and starting to prepare for the day. The bakery shop was the first to open and a wonderful smell of freshly baked bread wafted out from the front door every time someone opened it.

The early morning air was frosty and cold. There was a thin layer of ice over the windows of the cars and in the corner windows of the shops.

'Oh no, Zeno. LOOK!' Zula's face showed nothing but sudden complete horror.

'What is it? What is it?' panicked Zeno.

Magenta and Fusion's faces were now fearful of what Zula could see.

'Can anything now, go against us any further?' said Zula looking straight ahead at a lamp post.

They waddled over to see more clearly. What appeared to be glued onto the lamppost was a poster - a poster bearing a picture of the Evaders standing together in a row. Written above their heads and in big black bold print read: 'WANTED – ALIENS ON THE RUN!' The words written underneath deepened their nightmare: '$10 MILLION REWARD FOR CAPTURE. ALIVE PREFERABLE.' Under that, in very tiny writing, it read: 'conditions apply'.

The Evader friends looked at one another. Their nightmare was about to get worse still.

'Chin up Evaders.' Zeno said, trying to keep their spirits up 'No aliens will recognise us now. We must just find Electra.' Unbeknown to them, the poster they had seen was the first of thousands, many hundreds of thousands, all over the world...

Electra meanwhile, still lay fast asleep, snoring away and curled up snugly under the cardboard box, totally unaware of her capture for a reward of $10 million DEAD or alive.

The dream now was a more pleasant one than before. Even the thunderous noise in the distance and getting louder and louder as it came nearer couldn't wake Electra up. Its huge noisy presence dominating the surrounding area, as it travelled at a steady 5mph. A huge smelly bulk, its rear jaws snapping open, then shut, crushing to a pulp anything that was thrown inside it. So great was its size and dominance, it was blocking the road, and adamant not to let by any other passing body whether in a vehicle or on foot.

'Get out the way! Every bleeping week you do this!' came an angry yell from a motorist trapped from behind the monstrosity.

The huge tyres crept nearer to where Electra lay amongst the piles of rubbish, as it began to turn sluggishly into the alleyway.

Five pairs of alien legs walked briskly in a zig-zag fashion across the alleyway, picking up the dustbins and pouring its contents into the hungry jaws, every few seconds. Then they neared the pile of rubbish where sleepy Electra lay.

Meanwhile, it was such a pleasant dream. Electra and her four friends had managed to find their way back to the old volcano.

Many outstretched arms were ready to greet them with wails of joy and relief. Such a pleasant dream...

The giant tread of the tyres crept past the pile of rubbish and Electra's box, almost missing her curled up feet by just a few close inches. The concrete she lay on vibrated with the heavy presence now surrounding her.

As the noisy bulk crept by, the massive jaws of the eating machine stopped just past where Electra's sleeping body lay

'With any luck we should be done by twelve today!' said one of the aliens tipping another dustbin upside down. The alien's accomplice picked up the box with Electra inside and with strong arms and a throw, tossed it into the hungry jaws, crushing the box with such unrelenting force until a crumpled pulp and then swallowed into its enormous stomach.

'Yep. We're ahead of time today.' the reply came and brushed the back of his hand against his sweaty forehead. 'HONK ! HONK!' Still the horns continued from the irate queue of drivers stuck behind.

'I don't pay good money to be held up each week!' they yelled.

Chapter 25

The reality of having such a large bounty on their heads soon became even more apparent. The four desperate Evaders passed a television shop. As they each glanced into the window display showing the various television sizes from the fourteen inches to the giant sixty inches, were flashing pictures of the Evaders. One moment they would show the five friends as on the poster they had seen. The other flashes of pictures would show a mug shot of each Evader, giving a face on and sideways profile.

In-between those were reporters of all nationalities in various locations around the world reporting on the new alien phenomena. The Evaders couldn't look any more. This entire planet had gone insane.

They looked at each other in disbelief. Fusion shrugged his shoulders; the long red curls of his wig brushing lower against the white mohair cardigan-dress as it began to slip off the crown of his head.

'We must find Electra quickly. She will be in danger,' Zula said, raising her head up to reveal her worried eyes under the large furry zebra print hat with hanging earmuffs on either side.

'We do not have much time.'

As they continued to wander quickly down the street, they hoped that their nervousness did not show through their disguises.

'Don't wave your arms so much Magenta!' grumbled Fusion.

'You will draw more attention to yourself.' but Magenta ignored Fusion's words and exaggerated her movements even more.

As they sped further on, looking around them all the time for the sight of Electra or a cardboard box, they stopped outside a news stand. Neatly racked up outside the small sweetshop, the headlines all read the same:
'Close Encounters Of the $10 million Kind' screamed one.
'What's four feet tall and worth $10 Million? An EVADER!' announced another.
'ALIENS HAVE LANDED,' The Prime Minister confirms. So now the whole world knows...'
Another shocking headline in big bold letters read: 'Killer Aliens Escape! $10 Million Reward for Capture'. However, the most upsetting one read: $10 MILLION – DEAD OR ALIVE!' alongside a picture of the Evaders standing side by side.
'Why did we ever come to this planet? Zula asked, unable to take in the enormity of it all with the look of shock on her face.
The street now was slowly getting busier, the hostile aliens beginning to go about their day. It was rather a unique day now that there was so much excitement and anticipation in the air. Within just a few short hours, the news of the Evaders' escape had transpired into publicity frenzy, a mass hype. This became even more evident when to their astonishment, they thought they had seen Electra on the other side of the road.
'Look! There she is! THERE SHE IS!' cried out an excited Magenta but as they managed a closer look, a wave of horror crept over them. It was an alien but a smaller alien wearing what was an outfit resembling an Evader.

'How hurtful can they be?' Magenta was starting to cry, which was extremely rare as she was always such a happy character. Zeno, Zula and Fusion were feeling the hurt too. Their hopes had been set up and then dashed; it was a cruel irony.

'We continue our search. We'll find Electra, don't worry.' Zeno was struggling to be optimistic and tears began to form in his eyes. 'We move on.'

They must have wandered on for no more than a mere few minutes, when they heard lots of loud unnerving shouting coming from across the road. It was a group of young yobs looking for trouble.

'There they are.! GET THEM!' The six thugs start running over towards the Evaders, as they now each braced themselves ready for combat.

Suddenly, much to their utter amazement, they hear the thunderous running footsteps go past them and instead, jumped directly on top of a group of children dressed in Evader look-alike costumes. The Evaders, the real ones - decided enough is enough and rush off as quickly and as discreetly as they could whilst the chaotic scene a few metres behind them continued. No more than a minute later, when other aliens had decided to join in the fracas, the police arrived and intervened.

'This is a bad, bad world full of more Tridons,' said Zula. 'The sooner we get off this evil planet the better.' Never before had Zula spoken such angry words. It wasn't in her nature.

They continued their journey down the street. The aliens that passed them all looked on intently, however the real Evaders hidden under their disguises, were just passed off as being children wandering around, trying to get some sort of reaction.

'They haven't noticed us yet?' Fusion said quietly to Zeno.

But they will, sooner or later.

Chapter 26

What happened to you?' asked one of the many Evader faces that were crowded around. 'We have been looking everywhere. For many days now, we searched with our ships, not able to find you.'

Electra stood there and shrugged her little shoulders, looking somewhat lost and confused, even amongst familiar friends. Two of the Evaders, on noticing her vulnerability, went up to her and embraced her with a big hug.

'Welcome home,' they said. A smile and big happy eyes now swept over her relieved face. The comforting and reassuring arms around her once more, made Electra feel safe again. Finally, she was home, and now safe from any danger...

It had been a rude awakening. As she opened her eyes, no longer was there the surrounding comfort of the small box over her. It was gone.

As she awoke from the cold hard ground stretching her arms, the sense of vulnerability became real. As she looked up, she noticed all of the surrounding boxes and the bits full of over piling rubbish had gone.

In its place, were strewn bits of cabbage on the ground, accompanying empty cigarette packets and an empty can of baked beans.

The air felt cold and the sun was shining, adding just that little bit of warmth in-between the movements of the clouds above.

Electra got up from the cold ground. She failed to notice a piece of cabbage that had stuck to her backside, as she began to slowly wander off down the alleyway, she was unwittingly heading towards the main high street of the small town, totally unaware of the dangers now lurking ahead of her.

A stray dog with long scraggy hair trotted up to Electra, giving her a good sniff, which prompted Electra to stop moving instantly. The dog circled a now rigid Electra and on noticing the piece of cabbage stuck to her bottom, took hold of it in its mouth, and trotted off. Phew.

Looking down towards the end of the alleyway, Electra could begin to see the movements from the cars and a few humans walking one-way, and then another. Not sensing any immediate threat, she wandered further on. Leaving the quiet alleyway behind her, she turned into the more hustle bustle of the street.

Striding quietly along, looking around in all directions, this world with the aliens seemed so big. Noisy too, when the cars slowly drove past, stopping at moments to let the odd aliens cross the road.

Electra, now beginning to feel more awake, began to look upwards towards the tall alien faces that looked down at her as they rushed past. She was turning heads. On the other side of the road, she failed to notice other Evaders walking past, albeit without a distinctive bouncy gait, a few of which, were holding the hands of much taller aliens.

One Evader was being almost dragged along. It was crying, very distressed.

'I swear, if you don't stop that crying, you'll know it!' shouted the taller alien at the little being, and yanking away at its little hand.

Electra stopped outside the window of a small shop. The attractive and unusual display caught her attention. There were little animals running around cages, and jumping up with their front tiny paws up at the window, on noticing Electra's curious face peering through.

Electra wanted to see more, and decided to about turn and wander through the closed door of the pet shop.

Suddenly noises of chirping birds and the meows of kittens surrounded her. A rather bulky looking alien wandered towards Electra, its body covered in a large plastic apron covered in pictures of different breeds of cats and dogs.

The alien looked rather frightening to Electra, as the dark ash coloured hair was standing up on end as if the owner had suffered a massive electric shock. The untidy splurge of fluorescent pink lipstick didn't help its appearance either. It stopped right in front a bewildered looking Electra whose mouth had dropped open.

'Look kid,' it said. 'You can't come in here without an adult!' And with that, began to push Electra out the door! Feeling rather confused, she then continued to wander off again down the street. She bounded along for no longer than a few minutes, when all of a sudden, a large shiny black car pulled up alongside Electra with blacked out windows, which reflected everything around and promptly came to a stop. The passenger door side flung open, revealing an eager looking alien inside who was sitting at the driver's seat.

'Hey kid,' the deep male voice said creepily. 'Can I offer you a lift somewhere?'

The alien looked friendly enough, even if it did have a large black bushy caterpillar above its mouth, with matching jet-black dyed hair that was a harsh contrast against his very pale skin. Electra shrugged her shoulders. However, she now grew tired of wandering aimlessly around so lost, to the point that this offer appeared more than tempting. Maybe also, she thought, this alien could help her to find her friends?

Electra struggled into the front passenger seat which was quite difficult, as the vehicle was taller than a normal car, being an off-roader four-by-four. Electra now sat in the passenger seat, unable to see properly out of the window as she was much smaller than her strange alien companion. Her little legs dangled over the edge of the seat. The black-haired alien had a big smile on its face, revealing shiny yellow teeth, as it leant in the direction of Electra.

'That's better now, isn't it? Now, let's put this seatbelt over you.

We want to keep you safe now!' and with that, the alien leant over across Electra, a little bit too closely, its breath being quite smelly, actually and did the seatbelt up, clunking it firmly into place. Electra being that much smaller, had the edge of the seatbelt half strangling her as it went across. It was very uncomfortable.

The alien turned its smiling face towards the road ahead and with the engine still running and purring away, put it in gear and began to drive off.

They must have travelled no more than several hundred metres, just outside the edge of the small town, when Electra felt the vehicle turn and slow down, until it stopped outside what appeared to be a small depressing looking house. There were no other aliens around; the next house along was perhaps a hundred feet away, separated by a tall dark wooden fence.

The alien turned towards Electra, still smiling, and promptly undid his own seatbelt, still leaving Electra's tightly on. Then its voice seemed to change. 'Now then,' it said in a more serious tone. 'Let's take this mask off!' And with that, and much to Electra's alarm, it began to grapple away at the sides of Electra's face!

'How do you get this thing off?' The alien's voice was beginning to sound more impatient as it struggled.

'What off?' replied Electra in a loud voice, not amused.

'Your face off!' the alien snapped. 'I want to see your face!' And it began to grapple away again. Electra tried to swipe the large hairy hands away.

'This IS my face!' Electra yelled out loudly.

With that, the alien backed off, now looking somewhat startled.

'I am trying to find my Evader friends,' said Electra, now with a calmer voice.

'I have lost them.'

Now it was all beginning to click into place.

'I don't have just a child,' thought the kidnapper, 'but I have captured one of those EVADER THINGS!' The alien was determined to remain composed, even though now, sweat was beginning to show on his face, especially around the hairy caterpillar and on his brow.

'How can I help you?' asked the alien, its voice suddenly calmer and friendlier. Electra gave a big sigh, totally naïve as to the real intentions of the kidnapper.

'We were all trying to get back to the volcano, that is Zeno, Zula, Magenta and Fusion. Don't like Fusion much. He always moans.'

The kidnapper wiped the sweat from his brows with a handkerchief. His lack of composure was beginning to show, and his thoughts were already dwelling on what he would do with the $10 million reward.

'You say a volcano?' he asked. Electra began nodding away.

'That is where we Evaders are living now. It is a quiet and pretty place, with snow everywhere. We lost our home. We have to find somewhere new to live,' she said now shaking her head, feeling despondent with the way everything had turned out.

Not only had the alien captured a $10 million Evader (or so he thought) but it also had a rough location as to where an entire Evader population could be.

This was so much to take in all at once, and the alien's heart began to have palpitations, such was the excitement he was feeling.

Without anything further being said, the alien then jumped out of the driver's seat, slamming the door behind it. Electra was feeling bewildered now, and there was a strange noise as the central locking system clicked into place.

The kidnapper now unlocked the front door of the depressing and almost derelict looking house, and pulled out a mobile phone from inside the pocket of his black leather jacket.

'Police, yes,' he asked with his voice trembling.

'The Police here. How can we help you?'

'I've got one, it's in my car. I'VE GOT ONE!'

'I'm sorry, sir. You've got what? Speak slower.'

'AN ALIEN! I've got one of those aliens from the telly! It's in my car!'

Suddenly, the voice on the other end of the phone covered the receiver with its hand, so as not to be heard.

'Yep we've got yet another crank caller...' said the police officer, rolling his eyes at his colleague who was standing beside him. 'Right then sir. Where are you exactly?'

'192 Crankshaft Drive, Bonnington. There's a black four-by-four parked outside. I've locked the alien inside it.' The kidnapper's voice was almost gasping for breath. 'When do I get my reward...?'

'Let's deal with one thing at a time, please sir. The authorities are now on their way.' With that the phone went dead. The kidnapper went back outside, and stood by the vehicle. Peering discreetly and nervously inside, it noticed that Electra just sat there, her seatbelt still done up, almost looking like an obedient child waiting for further guidance. With big rather sad eyes, Electra looked up at the alien, as if waiting for the next instruction.

Then the sounds of sirens in the distance grew louder and louder and louder. They had arrived.

Chapter 27

Electra, unable to move, could only hear the screech of brakes and the sirens stop, then all of a sudden to see alien faces peering at her through the windows all around. Their faces were squashed up against the glass, their hands clasping around their faces, straining to see inwards due to the blacked out windows.

Now alarmed, Electra tried to crawl through the tightness of the seatbelt and managed to curl her body onto the floor of the car, hoping they couldn't see her.

Electra had tried to open the doors to the strange vehicle but they were all locked from inside.

'I've locked it in. It can't escape. Does this mean I get my reward?' the kidnapper asked the police officers.

'One thing at a time, please, sir.' With that, the kidnapper was almost pushed to one side, as if he was simply in the way.

Then in the distance, more sirens could be heard, and more screeching of brakes. This time, the smartly suited special branch agents took their turn to squint up through the black secrecy car windows, their eyes darting around trying to see Electra who was crouched low on the floor.

'Why are they looking at me?' cried Electra to herself.

'Why won't they leave me alone?' her frightened face peered upwards and her big eyes were watering with fear.

'What if they try to hurt me.?

Electra tried to hide herself even further under the glove compartment box and hoped they would all go away and leave her alone. The sound of the central locking system undid itself and before Electra could react, from both directions a series of gloved hands shoved themselves towards her, trying to grab hold of an arm or a piece of her tunic... the hands were snatching away as Electra struggled but her struggle was in vain. The hands were big and strong almost enveloping the sides of her small body as she was almost yanked out of the car as if she were a naughty child, kicking away.

What appeared to be the biggest strongest alien she had yet seen, a big burly man, smartly dressed in a dark navy suit, with swept back yellow hair and the most serious look on his face. With huge strong arms outstretched Electra was left dangling almost in mid air, her slender short legs frantically kicking away. Electra was being carried towards the open doors of yet another padded van.

For a moment, Electra froze, her body now rigid with fear. For when she looked inside the van, there were no Evaders, no friends this time to greet her, to reassure. She was alone, and this scared her even more. In quite a rough fashion as if she was some sort of a disgusting object, Electra was almost dropped inside at arm's length onto the floor of the van. With a loud slam, the rear doors of the van shut tightly closed, engulfing Electra in near darkness, the sound of keys and bolts followed.

With Electra now captured, attention turned to the kidnapper whose patience by now, was beginning to wear a little thin.

'I WANT MY REWARD! You owe me!' he said loudly, throwing his arms around.

'What do you know sir?' one of the smartly suited Special Agents asked.

The man began to calm down somewhat, trying to regain his composure, brushing his false hair with his hand as if trying to tidy up his appearance.

'I know where they are. It told me.' remarked the creepy man.

'What are you talking about?' a stern voice replied.

'Those Evaders. You know, the aliens. The thing told me where they are hiding!' The Special Agents looked at one another with wide eyes. With nothing further being said, the Agent suddenly produced a pair of handcuffs from inside her jacket, and with no hesitation and no rights read out to the creepy man, promptly clasped his hands together behind his back, clicking the handcuffs firmly into place.

'HEY! HEY! What the heck are you doing? Where's my reward? I'VE HELPED YOU GUYS!' With that, he was impatiently led towards a smart dark blue saloon car, and sat wedged tightly in between an agent either side of him on the back seat.

'I WANT TO MAKE A PHONE CALL! I have my rights you know! You can't arrest me! I'VE DONE NOTHING WRONG!!' All his flustered words were in vain as he was being completely ignored. As the car sped off at speed following the dark blue van in front containing a very frightened Electra, the kidnapper still went on.

'YOU JUST WAIT! When I get my reward - you'll be sorry! You won't have jobs – I'LL SUE!'

He just wouldn't shut up and so the agents had no other choice but to place a loose Blag Bag over his head, the inside of which was lined with an aromatherapy oil to help calm him down.

Both captives were taken to the nearest police station, which was a temporary and inadequate place to hold such a valuable cargo. Although the premises were far from ideal, the surrounding security around Electra was extremely tight.

The van and convoy slowed down and after stopping for a few seconds waiting for a security barrier to go up, the series of vehicles stopped in the quiet courtyard beyond. Staring out of the windows dotted around were many curious faces, who not knowing what was

138

happening and strictly were not to be informed, wondered if some major criminal had been caught, such was the commotion going on below in the courtyard.

Electra was totally oblivious to what was going on and now felt afraid of not only ever not seeing her fellow Evaders again but she was worried for her life, as she was now at the mercy of these nasty unpredictable aliens.

The rear doors of the van flew open, blinding Electra's eyes with the light. A heavy presence jumped inside with her, such was the instant downward motion of the van, only for Electra's head to be suddenly covered with a blanket thrown over her, her big green eyes still closed.

The blanket felt tight and suffocating over her and she had trouble trying to open her eye lids and long lashes. Electra began to panic even more. What were they doing?

Her body felt rigid and was now violently shaking. Large hands grasped her towards the rear of the doors and down the sloping ramp. So many curious faces from the windows strained to see this major criminal that had been caught, only to see a petite figure emerge walking in a bouncy fashion covered by a dark grey blanket. All station personnel were firmly instructed to stay where they were, such was the tight security but on seeing such a tiny almost strange shaped figure emerge and dwarfed by the towering presences around, only increased their curiosity further. They had no idea that an Evader had been caught.

The walking convoy headed towards a quiet room on the ground floor, the door closing behind them, heavily guarded on either side's by plain clothed officers and Special agents. Electra was slightly relieved to be picked up and placed onto a softly padded chair and held the sides of it firmly with her hands as if for comfort. The blanket thankfully was pulled off from Electra's head but as her eyes tried to open, she had trouble adjusting to the sunlight that was glaring upon her face. On noticing her pained expression, the agents turned the blinds at the windows down. The room grew darker now and only a small piece of sunlight appeared through the gaps, creating specks of light on the large wooden table in front.

Electra opened her eyes, which now darted around the strange new surroundings. Smart suited agents stood all around, their legs slightly apart, their hands gently clasped in front of them standing as if guarding a nightclub door. One prominent looking alien in particular was pacing up and down the room, starring continuously at Electra who looked like a naughty child in the big chair.

The alien had Electra's full attention now as her big green eyes followed him pacing around. Then he stopped looking directly at Electra who was looking less frightened than before, although still shaking, partly due to the room being cold.

The alien then turned around towards the others, feeling the cold himself.

'Isn't there any heating in this lousy building?' he asked impatiently. The Special Agents shrugged their shoulders, until one of them went over to check whether the radiators were on, which they weren't, then turned them on.

'Now then.' asked Special Agent Burnell, who now sat on the edge of the table in front of Electra.

'We understand you are frightened. We want to help you. You do understand me?' Electra reluctantly nodded. Whatever it was these aliens wanted, it was so imperative that Electra didn't tell them where the other Evaders were all hiding.

It would be the end of them all for sure.

A cup of warm frothy hot chocolate was placed in front of Electra by another agent who suddenly entered the room.

'Cold in here, isn't it?' he said, rubbing his hands together.

The alien sitting on the table, arms folded once again gained Electra's attention.

'We see you are in need. What can we do to help you?'
His voice was trying to be soft and understanding.

Electra thought hard for a moment, she was feeling vulnerable and alone. 'I want to be with my friends.'

'Yes, of course you do. You must miss them?'

'Oh yes. I do miss them so very much,' Electra replied.

'Do you know where they are?'

Electra shook her head. 'I have lost them…'

Unbeknown to Electra, in another room across the corridor, the kidnapper was also being questioned, the Special Agents offering the $10 million reward to him for information on what he knew.

'You help us find them, and you'll be a rich man,' promised Special Agent Nixon.

'What guarantee do I have? I can tell you what I know and I STILL WON'T GET MY MONEY!' the kidnapper said, his face sweating and his arms again waving about impatiently. There was a silence.

Agent Nixon produced a cheque book from inside his breast pocket, placing it on the table in front, followed by a shiny silver pen. With no hesitation, he signed there and then a government-funded cheque for $10 million.

Ripping it from the stub, Agent Nixon waved it teasingly in front of the man's wide excited eyes.

'What have you got to tell me?' he asked and with a serious stare, his eyes were firmly fixed on the sweaty informant. If ever there was ever such a tempting offer, this was it. The look of desperate temptation swept over the kidnapper's face, his mouth fell open and silent such was the surprise. Agent Nixon continued to wave the cheque around in a tantalising fashion, the kidnapper's eye's following his every move.

'This will be yours if you tell me where they are hidden?'
Now Agent Nixon was the one getting sweaty and impatient.

The kidnapper shook his head.

'No, I'm not buying it. It's a trick, you've no intention of giving me anything. I'll tell you where they are and then I'll STILL get no cheque.' He said adamantly.

Agent Nixon was taken aback, very surprised.

'Very well. We'll do this the hard way.' He said 'Either you tell us where those aliens are, or we'll slap as many allegations of unsolved child abductions on you faster than you can say bounced cheque.'

The Kidnappers mouth fell open totally speechless.

'I'll ask you one more time…'

'A volcano. The alien mentioned a volcano. With snow all around.'

They're living at the bottom of it, until they move on. It must be an extinct one.' Agent Nixon smiled a sly smile and then turned around to the next agent standing behind him.

'Right. We search every dormant volcano around. Inform General Storm.' said agent Nixon.

'Oh and Bob,' he continued, 'I think now we can close those child abduction files for the last ten years,' he said looking directly at the kidnappers shocked face.

'I think we can say we have found our man…'

The subtle interrogation of Electra in the adjacent room was suddenly interrupted by an abrupt loud knock on the door. It was followed by a rather excited Special Agent who almost stumbled in and breathlessly struggled to get the words out.

'We've caught them! THE ALIENS!'

Agent Burnell stood up quickly on hearing such news.

'Where? WHERE?!' he asked impatiently.

The Special Agent took a deep breath. 'Just outside the edge of town by Bentt Auto Sales. Four of them by the looks of it…'

Chapter 28

Zeno, Magenta, Zula and a very dishevelled looking Fusion crouched down as low as they could behind the small row of parked vehicles, hoping that they hadn't been noticed too much after all.

Above their heads, the large rusty sign displaying 'Bentt Autos' squeaked backwards and forwards in the wind, rather irritatingly. If only Magentas long wig and floppy white straw hat hadn't have slipped off, falling to the ground unexpectedly, then perhaps the sudden curious attention from the aliens passing by wouldn't have happened. The fact that ten curious faces stopped and stared at the alarmed Evaders, was not further helped by Magenta's irritated response. Almost in an act of annoyance, she shook her entire body erratically on the spot and with a high pitch yodelling sound in her attempt to scare them off, only drew even more unwanted attention.

From the moment they wandered a few hundred metres or so taking them just outside the edge of the small town, the Evaders had an uncomfortable sense they were being followed, being watched. The aliens walked slowly behind them as if keeping a safe distance, talking quietly away into their mobile phones. Magenta's erratic response had given themselves away to face the authorities who now surrounded them in the now deserted small garage courtyard. Their backs almost up against the set of double red wooden garage doors provided them at least with some protection from behind. In front however, separating them from the enemy was an old classic mini cooper, a tatty Mr Softee's ice cream van and an old bright rusty orange Beetle.

The assortment of police cars and vans seemed to grow in numbers by the minute.

'Come out slowly with your hands on your head! We will not harm you!' there came a sudden loud tannoy announcement from the chief armed personnel. It was obvious at this stage that the police were not used to dealing with this sort of alien presence.

'Get ready to shoot with the sleep darts - aim for the legs if you can - remember we want to get them ALIVE!' ordered the chief to his officers over the hand radio sets.

Their rifles were positioned ready to fire on the slightest movement made in the direction of the Evaders.

'Can you see anything Fusion? Magenta asked. 'Go and take a look.' Fusion gave a disgruntled look at Magenta and then reluctantly raised from his sitting position and up onto his feet. It was just as well they had positioned themselves behind the old ice cream van and sat directly behind the set of wheels so as not to be seen. Now Fusion stood up, he was still fortunately out of view from the many police who were now rigidly posed to shoot.

'CAN YOU SEE THEM?' Zula's poor attempt to whisper was so loud, even the police could hear what she was saying.

'SHUUSSSHHH!' replied Fusion so loudly back at Zula and once again the police could hear, to which they smiled wryly.

Fusion began to slowly creep to the edge of the ice cream van, ready now to move his head around and have a good look at the now vast police presence. Suddenly, a noise could be heard in the distance, which was getting louder by the second, a low rumbling sound. It belonged to a convoy of army vehicles and personnel and as the police all perched behind their cars and vans turning

144

around behind them to look, they could now make out the blackness of their silhouettes as they fast approached. The dusty ground below their feet vibrated, creating the tiny stones to jump up and down creating little clouds of dust as one by one, the noisy roar and intimidating dark green vehicles pulled up just behind the row of police cars and vans.

The Evaders now were feeling particularly threatened as they were completely cornered.

'What is this now, what do they want from us?' Zula spoke distressingly.

'I will take a look?' said Fusion who got down on his hands and knees and crept behind the edge of one of the wheels to take a look. Fusion's timing couldn't have been better, as all the armed police officers were for a second, looking over their shoulders towards the army personnel.

'What can you see, Fusion?' whispered Zeno.

'There are so many of them. We are trapped. We will not escape now...'

The others looked back at Fusion, sadness and defeat now etched on their faces.

'Let our Evader Betters protect us,' replied Zeno, looking up at the sky for a glimmer of hope.

Now the huge overpowering assortment of both police and the army dominated the surrounding area, totally encircling the Evaders at some one hundred metres radius. In a last gesture of affection, the Evaders one by one kissed both of their hands, then turned their palms around towards the others, moving them around in circular movements as if blowing each other a last farewell kiss. The moment they had always dreaded had once more arrived, and this time there really was nowhere to hide. Their time had come. Peaceful by nature, the Evaders wanted to avoid any confrontation with alien enemies.

As some of the military personnel jumped down from their vehicles, one person in particular stood out amongst the others as he emerged heavily from his chauffeur driven car.

It was the big, thunderous looking General Storm, the sweatiness of his skin, again shiny and angry covered in sweaty anticipation with his assortment of medals which were a colourful array, protruding outwards from his broad chest. His sudden presence intimidated all those around him and especially those that did know him. Those that did not, soon would.

General Storm and his subservient entourage behind him, hurried quickly up to those in charge of the current police operation.

'I'm General Storm,' He said his voice very deep and low.

'I'm Chief Commander Cherry. I'm in charge of this operation.' Replied the adamant, almost proud reply, also with his head held high and proud.

General Storm smiled a rare sarcastic smile.

'You are NOT now!' he said firmly and instantly turned his broad back on the bewildered Police Chief who in his shock was left utterly speechless.

'Did you do what I asked you to do with that one we had caught?' General Storm asked one of his military henchmen.

The man quickly nodded in response. 'Yes sir. All taken care of. It's gone now that we don't need it anymore.'

'GOOD!' came the blunt reply. 'Only these four more left to sort out. Make sure it doesn't take long. I want them GONE!'

'YES, SIR!!' The man saluted and then hurriedly marched off.

Chapter 29

Once again, there came a loud announcement from over the tannoy system:

'COME OUT WITH YOUR HANDS ON YOUR HEAD. YOU HAVE NO ESCAPE. WE WILL NOT HARM YOU. WE WILL PROTECT YOU.'

The Evaders knew the aliens could not be trusted. However, the Evaders were now cornered and vulnerable in their current position and had to do something NOW.

'I have a plan.!.' remarked Zeno excitedly, the others looked on intently at Zeno, waiting for the next instruction. 'Evaders – we will Unite – Not Fight.!'

Excited and newly charged with energy, the Evader's all stood up together, promptly holding up their own Glugers high above their heads, each one firmly touching together in a gleaming silver pyramid of brilliant light, with the Planet Evaders shouting together:

'POWER AS ONE!'

Within a blinding white flash of light, they were instantly transformed from their petite 4ft tall figures, to 7ft tall strong and athletic statues of muscle and agile power. The Planet Evaders now stood proud and imposing, their feet now stood apart in a powerful stance, ready to pounce with bounding new energy upon their hostile enemy.

In that split second however, something had caught the attention of General Storm's eye and it wasn't the blinding white flash emulating from the Planet Evader's instant power transformation.

He stood stiffly upright, pushing his enormous chest out in the process, knowing he was securely reassured behind the armed military personnel who were poised to jump into action at any moment.

The police officers by this time had been ordered to stand to one side – much to the frustration and annoyance of the Police Commander.

'It was nothing,' thought the General to himself, looking back ahead towards where the Evaders were about to emerge in a new powerful surge of bounding energy.

Suddenly, there was a loud 'WHHOOOHHH!' sound and a huge black shadow swept itself over the dusty ground in front of everyone causing alarm. Whatever it was, it happened in a flash of a second.

Everyone strained their eyes to look in an upwardly direction but whatever it was, it was gone. However, as they looked further around in the distance, something on the horizon in the sky began to appear. What at first appeared to be dozens of small black dots, gradually grew larger as they got nearer and nearer – as if a gigantic attacking swarm..

THEY WERE SPACE CRAFTS! A glimmer of hope swept over the Evaders. Their prayers had been answered. It was the Evader population, their friends, who had at last discovered them. They were going to be rescued. To be safe!

But wait. No... something was wrong.

As all the military, police and the Evaders looked up, now entranced staring up at the sky, as the ships appeared nearer still, they suddenly sensed a negative heavy atmosphere all around – as if a major storm was approaching - an uncomfortable feeling that perhaps this was a hostile invasion of some kind.

Suddenly it happened. Almost in a dark wave, as if a black cloud had come over the surrounding area, swept quickly over with a giant down thrust of microburst energy, that quickly disappeared sending the military, Police and the Evaders included, crashing to the ground with alarm. The accompanying thunderous noise shook everyone to the bone - a very fast and deep chugging sound, as if these objects were powered by an en masse of polluting black diesel smoke, that was about to run out and crash.

Now all of the attention was focused off of the Evaders themselves - and onto this new threatening sudden alien presence!

This invasion from nowhere was not that of the Evaders after all and unfortunately for the Evaders, they recognised instantly who they were....

The Tridons. They were the ruthless killing alien race who took no mercy for any living being and the ones who so ruthlessly invaded and destroyed their planet away from the Evaders. The Tridons were not satisfied enough that they already had the Evaders' home but also wanted to destroy them. Their mission and intended targets were as yet unfinished. This was it.

Now the Evaders had an additional enemy to face.

As all eyes continued to look upwards, the large cloud of enemy circled around in the distance and then on a straight course, again heading for those down at the garage.

This time as they approached, their presence was more menacing than before; the fast chugging sound grew louder still, as this time round, they were heading even lower. As the dark poisonous cloud began to swoop over their heads once more, everyone on the ground – Evaders included, ran this time for cover. Then the ships had started firing! Bright orange and red laser beams as quick as a strike of lightening, flew through the air in all directions, exploding into a ball of flame with anything it came into contact with.

General Storm, his heavy bulk struggling to move so quickly, tried at the same time to shout out orders and stumbled to catch his breath.

'SOMEONE GET THE EVADERS - GET THE EVADER'S!' he yelled but no military personnel were listening, as they continued running as far away from the garage as possible to take cover amongst the next buildings, which were at least a hundred or so metres distance away.

Once there, the military personnel scrambled back into their vehicles and drove off, away from the garage site. As they attempted to escape, they made easy large moving targets for the Tridons storming overhead.

The black cloud formation again swept in for another attack at the garage, their laser beams firing indiscriminately below. Then, there came a most incredible explosion!

A gigantic mushroom cloud of flame blew up into the air, the sound of which was deafening as if a huge bomb going off. The heat generated was immense - it could be felt by those who were still frantically trying to run away. Those that were nearer to the exploding garage still, were thrown violently to the ground.

The Evaders were also thrown, such was the enormous energy from the explosion from the row of petrol pumps below.

The Tridons, inside their dark metallic ships chuckled heavily away to themselves such was their joy, as they did so, they released a cloud of stinking sulphur from the pores of their scaly bulbous bodies.

The Evaders meanwhile, managed to get up from the ground. As they looked around them, they could see both military and police vehicles speeding along in all directions, in their panic to escape. General Storm had managed to assemble some of the military vehicles that had rocket launch power attached to them, to start firing upwards at the spaceships that again began to swoop around like a swarm of bees for the next attack. This time however, the military that was remaining, were ready and determined, the rocket launchers and machine guns mounted ready to fire upwards.

The chugging sound grew deafeningly loud as once more, as the spaceships swept over the open spaced exposed area like a huge black cloud, only this time and unexpectedly, to come under intense fire from those below. The Tridons unprepared for such a response knew that the Evaders never fired back when attacked in the past and now were caught off guard, now made for easier targets this time for the military.

The deafening sounds of both laser fire and rocket launchers going off, each exploding into a ball of flame and flying metal in all directions, only resulted in the most hideous scene of destruction.

Such was the force of the military vehicles being hit by laser fire, that they flew into the air like tin cans, the spaceships had also been hit with such surprising force, knocking them instantly from their firm flying positions, and causing them to fall out of control and at a steep angle towards the ground, most of which exploded into flame upon impact.

The entire scene now resembled a battle zone. General Storm, standing on the back of a rocket launcher truck that yet hadn't been hit, ordered through his radio set for air force jets to immediately intercept the enemy left above and shoot them down, something he should have done sooner. His voice through the radio set was one of sheer anger but the recipient's voice on the other end at the control base, was also shaky.

The Evaders were surrounded by burning destruction as just a short distance from them, were many burning wreckages of the military vehicles, with flames so intense, everything that was once inside, was gone.

General Storm now decided to ignore the remaining, smaller cloud of ships in the distance, which once again turned around at a steep flying angle ready to continue the firepower below.

His attention now was focused on one thing only - to destroy the Evaders. From the raised platform of the truck, he looked around a total 360 degrees in his attempt to locate them.

Sure enough, his squinting paid off when he spotted them just alongside one of the burning vehicles, its black smoke billowing in an upwards spiral in the wind.

With no hesitation, General Storm banged his hairy fist fiercely on the roof of the military truck, the sudden loud noise alarming the driver in the cab who was waiting patiently for the next instruction.

'TURN 60 DEGREES WEST – NOW, YOU IDIOT!' he bellowed.

'YES SIR!' the startled reply came. The driver was in some form of shock and whilst he clung almost hanging over the steering wheel, his head and his eyes were peering only upwards unaware of the burning wreckage of a Tridon ship straight ahead that they were on a crash course for.

General Storm could see this, but the driver couldn't. Once again, he banged his fist so hard on the roof of the cab trying to alert him to the danger ahead, that he had started to break the bones in his hands, such was his determination and anger.

'STOP THIS TRUCK!' he shouted.

But the driver was in some sort of a trance. General Storm took matters into his own painful hands and leaning precariously over to the side of the driver's cab, managed to grab hold of the steering wheel, instantly turning it away from the burning mass right in front of them.

It worked. The truck swung violently over to one side avoiding the collision, however so sudden was the turn to the side, that the vehicle began almost in slow motion, to turn on its side on two wheels until with a heavy thud, it landed violently, the front and side windows shattering on impact.

General Storm was instantly thrown out of the rear of the truck, almost like a rag doll, such was the force, his bulky body turning over and over on the dusty ground.

His once immaculate uniform was now covered head to toe in dust, resembling a ghost like image.

The truck itself skidded along on its side in one long straight line and was heading directly to where the Evaders stood, their eyes transfixed on the mass of metal out of control as it ploughed towards them with speed.

The Evaders leapt 20 feet into the air to avoid the collision. Then literally six feet from where they landed, the monstrosity came to a sudden stop in a large cloud of choking dust, so narrowly missing them.

The Evaders coughed loudly away, as the wind direction blew the dust over their heads.

'NEARLY HAD US!' spluttered Magenta.

It was best that they didn't speak too soon, as General Storm now just several metres away, began to stumble clumsily to his feet, his eyes solely transfixed on the Evaders, his ghost like face contorted with anger. Then the thunderous bulk staggered heavily towards them…

Chapter 30

It all happened very quickly. Just as General Storm's angry bulk headed at a determined pace towards the Evaders, a flurry of military vehicles appeared out of nowhere, instantly firing an ejector net of Graphene at the Evaders, instantly pinning them to the ground, under a criss-cross netting of the most strongest metal in the world.

As the Evaders looked around, they were eclipsed by the military presence. Large, dark and menacing, so much so, the light around them almost seemed to disappear.

The Evaders were trapped and in the suddenness of it all, they were unable to leap out of the way quick enough, or to even reach their Glugers in time.

To make matters worse, the Evaders had suddenly returned back to their usual small frames, due to their power formula waring off in the limiting time of only a few minutes.

Now guns pointed rigidly above their heads.

Outside the immediate circle surrounding them, the battle continued. The remaining army presence fired their machine guns and antimissiles at the alien spaceships, as they continued to swoop down from every direction. The noise all around was deafening.

'GET OUT OF THE WAY! LET ME GET THROUGH!' General Storm ordered loudly above the noise, his bulk trying to squeeze through in-between two parked military vehicles together, almost getting stuck.

As General Storm now stood there, panting out of breath and too close for comfort hovering above the

Evaders, he could touch them if he wanted to, they were that close.

Even though all eyes and guns focused closely on the trapped alien beings, the soldiers couldn't help but keep glancing at anything else outside the circle that moved or made for an easy target for the swooping attacking spaceships. The military around them continued to have a job on their hands trying to avert the enemy lasers from the immediate scene.

'YOU'VE ESCAPED ME ONCE – YOU WILL NOT ESCAPE ME AGAIN!' he bellowed. His dust covered black bushy eyebrows met in the middle; he had now sweated so much, revealing a menacing shiny face.

'GET ME THE HELICOPTER!' he bellowed an order.

'GET THEM TO THE NARKSIS BASE - NOW!' The order was quickly radioed through to the control room. Within what seemed a long three minutes, a dark green military helicopter appeared, landing just outside the circle that surrounded the alarmed captured Evaders.

The dust produced from the effects of the rotor blades, once more covered everything and anything around, including General Storm, and he tried to protect his eyes from the flying dust with not much success.

The Evaders closed their eyes tightly to protect them from the flying dust.

'Stay silent and calm.' remarked Zeno to Magenta, Fusion and Zula. 'We'll get through this.'

Suddenly, the metal net that was tightly pinning the Evaders to the ground, was released. It was such a relief for them, as the tightness of the thin metal netting, had left indented patch work lines on their faces. Within a split second, military hands confiscated their precious Glugers from their holsters.

The swirl of the helicopter blades began to slow down and the noise of the engine grew low. Two of the vehicles reversed out of the way, making a path for the Evaders and their escort to take them to the helicopter.

'GET INSIDE!' ordered the general, pointing a stocky finger towards the door that had slid open for them.

Zeno, Zula, Magenta and Fusion clambered up the couple of steps and into the helicopter, taking their seats. One of the military personnel, then buckled in each Evader, as firmly and attentively as he could, securing each one in a seat harness. This was invaluable cargo.

The side door slammed shut. Once more the engine roared itself up, the rotor blades soon to turn so quickly as if a blur.

The helicopter quickly raised up from the ground, revealing to the Evaders a clearer picture of everything that was still happening. They could still see the evil space ships zooming around in all directions, flying so quickly and with a loud rattling sound as if each one was about to fall apart.

Laser beams of reds and oranges continued to fly in all directions, exploding into flames and every object it touched was a dreadful sight. Soldiers were the immediate targets, being the ones moving around in all erratic movements in an attempt not to be hit. However, many below were not successful to the upset of the Evaders, as well as their armed escort and the helicopter pilot whose head was turning frantically in all directions. The pilot appeared to be getting more panicky, as sweat was pouring from his face with the erratic movements his head made, trying to react quickly to what was going on around the helicopter.

To make matters less reassuring, the pilot now began to make rather unnerving movements with the joystick resulting in the helicopter making uncomfortable and unpredictable turns to the left and right.

The Evaders and the escort held the sides of their seats firmly, which was almost in vain, as they seemed to slide about in all directions, even though they were very securely fastened in.

'MISSED ME! WHOOHHH!' the pilot was saying, his voice shaking with the vibration the helicopter was now making. Still the laser beams flew around, and now the helicopter began to swerve erratically up and down as well as side to side. It was an out of control roller coaster ride.

'I want to get off NOW!' Fusion yelled.

'MAKE IT STOP! STOP – STOP!' shouted Zula at the top of her voice. 'Hold on,' said Zeno. 'We will land in a moment.' But even he was scared as they had no control whatsoever.

Even if the helicopter wasn't hit by laser fire, it sounded as though it could suddenly break up in mid air. The engines noise was groaning loudly, as if struggling now for power, it had been tested to its absolute limits

'BANG!' There was a deafening explosion which violently rocked them all sideways. The helicopter engine was making a high-pitched squealing sound as if hit. It was badly damaged.

'NO - NO! WE'RE GOING DOWN! WE'RE GOING DOWN!' screamed the helicopter pilot and frantically took hold of the joystick with both hands trying to regain some sort of control but now they were spinning. Around and around and around. Everything outside the windows became a blur. The gravitational pull as they fell, still spinning quickly around, pinned each one on board firmly rooted to their seats. The pressure felt so heavy on one side of their bodies, they were unable to move.

The directional force of the falling helicopter paralysed them and the deafening high pitch squealing sound from the engine seemed to echo through them.

The inevitable impact of the crash was yet to happen. Still falling… still spinning… can't move… this was it. Their hopes this time had run out, there was no escape. They couldn't even move. The pressure on each of their heads made them look through the windows on one side and although only a light blue hazy blur, was now turning a darker colour as they fell nearer to the ground.

Each one on board tried to brace themselves now for the inevitable crash that was about to happen. Their stomachs felt sick. They closed their eyes. Then the most enormous thud rocked them, they could feel the seats below them come away from their secure bolted positions, sending each of them flying in an unknown direction. The noise was so loud, then temporary deafness covered their ears and their eyes remained tightly closed, too terrified to open, the feeling all over them became surreal, as if it was a bad dream.

This was not really happening. Then it stopped.

Chapter 31

The helicopter had fallen like a stone from its position of only one thousand feet. It had landed heavily on its side, the giant rotor blades buckling against the ground, turfing up great mounds of earth and grass until the blades flew off into the air, just missing a few soldiers who had frantically thrown themselves onto the ground.

The Evaders still inside the helicopter tried to move, but couldn't. They could just about see the back of the balding head of the helicopter pilot, his helmet now had been pushed down low over his eyes and his head was hanging loosely downwards and his body slumped over to one side of his seat, which had come away from its rooted position and landed back down again but in the wrong place.

He wasn't moving. The soldier who was their escort couldn't be seen.

The Evaders tried to struggle loose, but they were each held down by the seats in front of them which had collapsed when the helicopter crashed. There were only thin streams of light peering through the inside of the helicopter now that the side facing upwards was badly damaged. Thick wavering clouds of dust particles could be seen through the strands of light. Zeno managed to free his arms and with nimble fingers, undid his seatbelt, which most definitely had saved his life. He turned to Fusion to undo his seatbelt too, which had somehow managed to wrap itself round Fusion's neck. Magenta's arms and legs were trapped quite badly, unable to move, but fortunately Zeno and Fusion between them managed to lift the collapsed seat just enough to release her, resulting in a groan of pain.

'You could have been a bit more gentle!' she said.

Then Zeno, Magenta and Fusion then turned to help Zula who was collapsed as if sleeping, totally silent and not moving.

'Zula are you with us?' asked Zeno gently giving her lifeless arm a prod.

There was no answer. Her small body was slumped to one side as if leaning towards the collapsed wall of the interior, her face turned away from them, her head hanging downwards. Both of her legs were firmly trapped by the other collapsed pilot's seat in front. Zeno gently took hold of the sides of her face with both hands turning it towards them. There was a cut on her forehead, her black hair just about concealing the head injury that would require urgent attention.

The others now very concerned, tried in vain to wake her and calling her name. Still there was no response.

Suddenly, they heard grunting noises coming from outside. It was coming from the near distance but gradually seemed to be getting louder on one side of the helicopter. The hole wasn't big enough to see enough detail as to what was heading towards them and could only make out a dark moving mass but not a particular outline. The grunting noise became louder still, and now a chilling feeling came over them. This was a familiar sound.

'I hope it's not!' said Magenta shakily.

They had a horrible feeling inside them. The Evaders became more unsettled and they had to be sure if their instincts were right.

Zeno noticed a larger gap in the collapsed helicopter, which was about four feet above their heads, and so very carefully and trying not to tread on the others, Zeno stood up taking hold of the back of the collapsed front seat for balance and aimed to look through the small gap no larger than a tennis ball.

'Oh no! NO! NO!' said Zeno, whose voice usually sounded so calm.

'What! WHAT!' Magenta asked impatiently. 'What is it..?'

Waddling heavily from side to side, the blubbering mass of stinking sulphur smelling flesh wobbled like jelly.

The distinctive smell was becoming more and more overpowering the grunting and groaning louder by the second. The ground beneath them began to vibrate such was this heavy presence coming for them.

The Evaders were totally unable to move. They were still trapped in this metal shell, unable to escape.

This was not a good situation to be in, especially that there was almost a full tank of fuel that unbeknown to the Evaders was ready to ignite at any moment. Worse still, each of their Glugers had been taken from them by the military. They had no power to defend themselves.

The farting sulphuric mass became overpoweringly near, its bodily steam creating clouds of mustard yellow whiff with each movement it made.

The Evaders now covered their noses with their clasped hands such was the suffocating stench from the outside and the smoke now developing quickly inside, Zeno covered Zula's nose and mouth with his hand in an attempt to protect her, not knowing if she was alive or not.

Suddenly to their alarm, the outside crushed shell of the smoking helicopter began to rock violently from side to side, as if the huge alien wanted those that were inside.

'GO AWAY!' shouted Magenta out loud.

'WE ARE NOT HERE!' Now the rocking shell of the broken helicopter, the noise deafening their ears, began to roll onto its roof, at the same time revealing a large gaping hole that could enable the Evaders to try to escape. Only problem was, the enormous ugly, scary looking mass of a

161

head, the size of which almost covered the four feet wide gap, its red and fierce looking menacing eyes, its large mouth open and angry revealing not only huge fang like dirty orange teeth but the stench of its breath took theirs away. Its tongue was so long almost touching them, covered with a thick acidic saliva that stung on impact as it dripped.

The Evaders yelled with more disgust than from fright.

Its tongue, the length of an ironing board, and the thickness of a pillow now dangling in and out of its huge ferocious mouth, and the Evaders tried to edge back so as not to gain contact with it. Adding to their horror, its mouth was covered in a thick sick like gunge that dripped onto the Evaders below.

Also crawling around on its tongue were large bug-like creatures the size of your hand, some appearing to have pincers and also long white maggots wallowed in the filth. Some of the creatures dropped on top of the Evaders themselves adding to their cries.

A fire was now gathering more ferociously and was quickly nearing the ruptured fuel tank of the helicopter. Once again the Tridon violently rocked the shell of the crippled helicopter, this time managing to throw the Evaders clear, as the side of the gaping hole fell apart into a flimsy mass, enabling them to now be clear of the burning wreckage. Zula was also thrown clear but her body now lay lifelessly still and vulnerable.

The Tridon was now on the other side of the helicopter and for a confused and impatient moment lost the sight of its prey. In the frustration, it started to thump the burning mass with its enormous scaly fists.

The Evaders grabbed the opportunity and between them, they managed to pick up Zula and in an awkward very slow fashion, began to rush away from the scene.

'Oh no! It's seen us! GO FASTER!' panicked Magenta, dropping Zula's legs to the ground as well as herself in her attempt at running backwards facing the Tridon. The suddenness of it all now stopped the Evaders from moving any further and they all fell to the ground. The Tridon was now ferociously angry with the Evaders who were some thirty feet away, began to make its heavy way around the burning wreckage that was now billowing black smoke, and towards the fallen Evaders.

Before the ferocious Tridon could make any distance from the helicopter, there came an enormous explosion that seemed to shake the entire area.

The Evaders bodies were almost thrown to the ground, such was the force. Pieces of burning wreckage landed around, narrowly missing them.

Now there was the smell of burning in the air, mixed with the stench of sulphur. It was a sickening smell but for the Evaders now, the immediate threat was over. The relief was evident on their faces.

Propping themselves up from the ground, they immediately noticed that the aerial attack from the Tridons had finished and now the air was silent and still.

As they looked around, surveying the potential hazards, they saw what appeared to be a crashed Tridon ship. It was lying on its side, at a slight angle but appeared to have no structural damage.

It was no more than a hundred feet away.

'I have an idea…' suggested Zeno glancing towards the craft. The others were mystified. Zula still lay motionless and the bleeding from her head had worsened. Whatever Zeno had in mind and if Zula was still alive, time was a luxury they didn't have.

Chapter 32

Each slow step they took towards the stricken Tridon ship grew harder and harder, the weight albeit not very much, of Zula's lifeless frame which grew heavier and heavier. They were determined to keep going. It wasn't much further now, no more than fifty feet away. Zula's skin colour had changed dramatically. From what was a healthy light orange skin colour of blossoming young cheeks, had turned grey, adding further to their worry, yet they still had to carry on.

If only for one moment they stopped and tried to listen for or feel a pulse, then they would know either way whether their struggling attempt would be vain.

At last they had reached the crashed ship. The abrupt impact it had made, created a tall mound of earth on one side, wedged at an angle of some 30 degrees. The outside plating of the ship was dark grey, with large overlapping scales like that of a crocodile covered all over it, the surface also being shiny and wet looking. Its shape almost resembled that of a giant spider, as underneath in its attempt to land, it produced a series of long crab like legs all around, albeit the ones round the other side were buried in the ground. There were also large bulbous windows that looked like giant eyes all around. On the outside they appeared black and mysterious as if wanting to disguise whatever it was inside, and as the sunlight shone down on their shiny polished surface, its reflection looked as if the eyes were alive.

The Evaders somehow, were determined to commandeer the ship. The only problem was they had to get into it but how, they didn't know.

They carefully laid Zula on the ground, and the sight of her condition prompted their determination even further. Each of the Evaders decided to bang loudly on the outside of the Trideon ship with their Gluger weapons.

'Hello, hello. Anyone in?' said Zeno patiently. No answer.

'That's not the way to do it,' replied Fusion abruptly, and tried his version. 'COME OUT NOW - UP YOUR HANDS!'

Electra's poor attempt didn't help very much either: 'Yes, we are big and nasty and you can't escape!'

The others viewed her small frame, each amused at all their physical contradictions and her timid voice.

Magenta however, decided to climb on top of the mounded earth and strained to look inside through one of the ship's eyes.

'I can see something,' she said. 'It is moving.'

Before any of them could do anything else, within a split second a scaly side panel to the ship suddenly flew open, causing Magenta to fall down with fright and the others to jump away. They were instantly hit by a thick cloud of dark yellow sulphurous gas, being the sheer stench from the evil alien Tridon inside. The smell was so bad, that the Evaders were temporarily paralysed by it, such was its overpowering stench.

They were left coughing and spluttering, trying to cover their nose and mouth until the vaporous poisonous cloud disappeared.

Now staring directly at them with large red angry eyes and gritted huge spiked teeth, was a terrifying Tridon.

The Evaders jumped back with alarm, expecting the hostile alien to attack them. Both to their relief and astonishment, it didn't.

165

Zeno noticed that the Tridon was injured, and quite seriously looking by the wound it was exposing on one side of its body, oozing out a thick red and orange like fluid.

'I don't think this one can move.' Zeno observed, still looking at the creature and slowly creeping forward. Magenta without any hesitation, picked up a handful of dust and dirt from the ground, flinging it unexpectedly at the alien's eyes.

The Tridon screwed its huge giant face up, closing its eyes from the reaction to the dust and gave out a very loud roar, waving its long scaly covered arms around in frustration. It was just as well the creature couldn't move, as the enormous claws on the end of each of its three fingers would probably have destroyed the Evaders.

Zeno decided to climb through the doorway and into the ship, much to the alarm of the others.

'No Zeno! No! NO!!' Magenta panicked, but Zeno was now already inside and keeping a safe distance from the angry Tridon who was perched injured alongside the other giant seat.

'I have an idea. We can get out of here.'

Zeno was studying the basic controls in front. They had to be basic, as the Tridons were perhaps the simplest of pre- alien intellectuals in the whole of the Galaxy.

'Come, come Evaders. Be careful with Zula,' said Zeno waving at the others whose heads were peering anxiously inside the ship.

Magenta and Fusion between them, struggled to pick up Zula, whose face had turned even greyer still.

'Careful now. Careful, slowly, slowly...'

They raised Zula just onto the inside of the ship. It had a most strange but comfortable surface to it, moving around like a waterbed, and it made strange slurpy noises with each slight movement.

'Now what?' huffed Fusion impatiently. 'That thing had better not come near me,' he moaned. staring back at the Tridon. The Tridon glared straight back.

'I'm going to get us out of here, Evaders. We shall try to find the others,' declared Zeno who with outstretched arms, reached over to the control panel in front, which consisted of a series of different sized bulbous circles in vibrantly bright colours. Suddenly the ship began to jump up and down violently on the spot, throwing the Evaders up and down from the seat. The Tridon let out a large chuckling laugh followed by a deafening smelly burp that added further to their discomfort.

'Clueless! That's what you are!' yelled Fusion loudly, his voice shaking with the violent shaking of the ship. Magenta tried to hold Zula securely down, not wanting to add further injury, even though they had a job stabilising themselves as the ship continued to jump up and down in short sudden bursts. Zeno struggled to press the luminous green bulge that was placed nearest to the Tridon, who seemed to be enjoying their struggling efforts.

With Zeno's arm now outstretched leaning over to try to press the green 'go' button, the Tridon - although unable to move, began to snap its enormous fangs towards Zeno's muscular but vulnerable arm.

'Zeno, NO!' cried out Magenta, alarmed, but Zeno had just managed to press the green bulge with all his might, and suddenly the ship not only stopped jumping erratically up and down, but also began to raise itself from the ground. The Tridon's face now looked furious and raging.

As the Evaders stared out through the large round windows, they could see that the ground now, was a thousand feet below them and they were able to see the small town and its people that had betrayed them.

In the distance straight ahead, they could see mountains, probably the wrong direction to go in but it seemed an inspiring idea to Zeno right at this moment.

Now taking hold of the rather large joystick in-between Zeno's seat and that of the angry Tridon, Zeno with determination and both hands, pushed the lever forward.

'WHOOSSHHH!' The acceleration was intense, throwing all the Evaders and the Tridon backwards in their seats. As they looked through the large bulbous window below their feet in front, they could see the land rush past under them so quickly, that everything was just a blur.

Their mission was to find the snowy capped mountains - wherever you are – HERE WE COME!!

Chapter 33

The mountains were now straight ahead of them and the Evaders could see on the horizon the highest mountain peaks, pointed and spectacularly white, almost glistening in the distant sun. The Tridon ship, although very fast travelling at around 500mph, still made a loud chugging sound as it continued its journey and every so often, yanking in a sudden backward movement, resulted in those on board being on a constant edge. To get this far had been a miracle in itself, and Zeno had noticed that only thirty minutes or so had passed since they had ventured off. Zeno also realised that it wouldn't take much longer for the ship to reach the snowy mountain range.

Since they had all originally ventured off in their mini whizzer ship in the first place, ready to explore this new planet, only for them to crash land so unceremoniously in the middle of a busy supermarket car park - they estimated that they couldn't have travelled that far a distance.

'I do feel sick…' Fusion began to moan, rubbing his tummy. Zeno ignored his moan knowing it was really just attention seeking because he was bored, and instead asked him how Zula was.

Zula's face had turned a stony grey white.

'I am worried, Zeno. I have never seen an Evader this colour before, and her face and hands feel so cold…'

Zeno was beginning to struggle now, completely drained at the thought of his sister and his best friend being no longer with them. The thought of losing both Electra and Zula would destroy their lives forever.

Zeno gradually began to increase the height they were chugging along at and saw that the snowy covered mountains on the horizon were looming fast.

As they began to fly over the rough terrain, they noticed the snow below appear sporadically in places, as if in the process of melting. As they gathered pace, a blanket of snow dominated the area as far as they could see.

Before they knew it, they were flying and chugging away over the mountains. It was a beautiful autumnal day with a brilliant light blue sky, the occasional wispy cloud moving slowly. Everything above and around them further highlighted the sheer beauty below, the sunlight glistening against the snow. These aliens on this planet, didn't deserve to live in such a spectacular environment. As the Evaders peered through the bulbous large windows down towards the floor, in front of them, they could see the unusual reflection that the Tridon ship was making. It was quite a hideous sight against its stunning surroundings, as if a giant flying insect.

If Zeno had remembered one distinctive thing about the volcanic hideout where their Trillion ship had crash landed, it had to be the spectacular shape that it was. Perfectly round was the very top of the caldera, the old extinct volcano, with sloping sides at a steep sixty degrees, the snow so perfect and immaculate as if covered by a white blanket. It was such an amazing sight.

Zeno remembered - for straight ahead of them, so prominent and proud was the spectacular cone shaped volcano, its great vastness dominating the entire area.

Finally, they had reached the one last place that could save them!

As Zeno slowed down for a careful approach, what seemed to be a sudden wave of disbelief had washed over Zeno, Magenta and Fusion. Up until now, their journey for so long, had been a nightmare and to now suddenly reach their goal and they hoped their saviour, seemed almost too good to be true.

Perhaps now their luck was about to change, they thought?

'Zeno - do you know - we have made home. We are safe,' said Magenta, the look of bewilderment evident on her face with her mouth wide open, smiling excitedly.

'About time too!' snapped Fusion. 'The thought of spending any more time with you would fill me with horror!'

Magenta screwed her face up at Fusion teasingly. Zeno, however, was very quiet, still concentrating on controlling the ship. It was still going to be a difficult if unpredictable manoeuvre to land the Tridon ship actually inside the dead volcano crater. Zeno certainly wasn't going to get any help from the stinking evil Tridon beside them, even if its life had to depend on it.

Zeno managed to slow the ship right down, chugging away even louder as it almost came to a stop, hovering over the edge of the enormous black caldera below them. From so high above as they looked through the bulbous windows by the floor in front, it was as if they were balancing on the edge of a giant cliff.

The blackness below appeared so vast and like the great unknown, an immense black hole ready to swallow you up, never for you to return.

'It doesn't look welcoming now, does it?' said Magenta peering down with anxious wide eyes. 'Are you sure we have the right one?' she asked Zeno, anxiously observing in all directions to see if a friendlier looking volcano was in sight.

'This is the one Evaders,' said Zeno with a serious tone of voice.

'Hold on. I don't know what I am doing… got to try to land this thing…' Zeno began scratching his wide forehead with one hand, the other at random began to push at the various large controls in front and letting go completely of the joystick. The joystick being the main control instrument with which to land safely by…

'No, it's not this one…' Zeno continued, experimenting with the controls.

The Tridon alongside him began to roar with laughter so much so, its body rippling away with its immense bulk, in the process letting off a cloud of yellow sulphurous choking gas, the smell of a thousand bottom burps.

Coughing and spluttering, there was no escape. The yellow toxic cloud filled inside of the ship, and now Zeno couldn't see what controls he should press, at the same time fighting for breath.

'ZENO! DO SOMETHING! QUICKLY!' Yelled out Magenta from behind 'CAN'T … BREATHE…!

In a rush of panic and not knowing what to do, Zeno suddenly grabbed the large joystick in front of him with both hands firmly clasped, and instinctively, yanked it downwards so desperately.

Suddenly, the ship started to fall into the black abyss below. The ship dropped like a lift unable to find its breaks, and the Evaders were yelling with panic. They were dropping so fast, that the air was almost taken from their lungs. Thankfully, only the ship's standard fitted harnesses, held them securely in place. The sulphurous yellow gas with the fall of the ship, now formed a thick cloud like layer against the ceiling.

As for the Tridon, although strapped awkwardly into its safety harness, the gravitational force pulled its head up against the ship's ceiling, immersing its own face in its own sickening odour.

The Evaders were still falling and their bodies still paralysed, but their minds trapped, each one only focused on one thing - the inevitable crash landing on those below. It would end in certain deaths and their many Evader friends now oblivious to what was about to happen…

'Pull up Zeno, PULL UP! Yelled out Magenta 'We will meet certain death!'

Zeno stared back with wide alarmed eyes. 'Locked into position... can't.... move,' he gasped struggling with the large lever trying to pull it with every ounce of strength. 'HOLD ON!'

Chapter 34

In a large cloud of dust, the Tridon ship crash-landed with such a hard thud, that all inside were thrown violently up out of their seats, even the stinking Tridon alien, who had also successfully managed to knock itself out, as its giant head had hit the ceiling. It was a good thing they were wearing their safety flight belts this time.

Zeno looked around at the others.

'All Evaders well?' They all nodded, but concern once more turned to Zula, whose body now looked limp and lifeless like a rag doll.

'Are we here, Zeno? Are we back home now with the others?' asked Magenta, who appeared to be in shock, probably caused by the hard impact, her head swinging around as if drunk. Zeno one by one, undid their safety belts and now with excited anticipation, leant over to the windows to peer outside.

'I can't see anything! Only dust!' said Fusion squinting with a squashed face against the mottled window. 'No, I can't see any Evaders...'

With some nervousness, Zeno and Fusion made their way over to the large doorway of the ship, the honeycombed see through glass appearing a dark rustic red against the volcanic wall outside, with a flickering effect from the flamed torches against the rock walls.

Placing each of their palms onto the claw shaped panels on either side, the large circular doorway opened up from the middle, spiralling around until it was fully open.

'AAHHH!' gasped Zeno peering outside the now exposed open space.

The Evader friends looked at each other and a smile came over their faces. Magenta stuck her head out into the open 'Hello! Hello! We are home! She yelled excitedly and started to jump up and down, expecting Evaders to appear from all directions. Both Magenta and Zeno's smiles diminished when they could hear nothing. Only silence.

Magenta once more flung her head outside the doorway.

'HELLO, ANY ONE HERE?' then quickly retreated when again, no response.

'What do you think has happened?' asked Magenta 'Have we accidentally killed them all?' she asked, with eyes looking downwards over the edge of the doorway as if to indicate they had landed on top of them. Zeno shook his head. 'No Magenta. Something else is wrong. Even if we have landed on many Evaders there would still be many more around. It looks as though they have left without us - GONE!'

There was only one way to find out. The Evader friends had to investigate. Perhaps they were all having a get together at the other end of the enormous caldera.

After all, the area itself being a huge mile or more across, would explain the possibility that perhaps their abrupt landing hadn't been noticed after all?

Suddenly, loud grunts and stinking burps came from the direction of the Tridon, as it quickly regained consciousness, its body beginning to release sulphuric gases once more now that it appeared to be in a disgruntled angry state.

'Quickly. Fusion. Grab Zula! Quickly it's woken up! It will gas you!

Fusion moved so fast, such was his panic, as he rushed to drag Zula away to safety. The Evaders assembled themselves very close to the doorway.

Zeno managed to release the ramp that appeared from under the floor in front of them and it gracefully touched the rocky ground some ten feet below.

Carefully taking hold of Zula's limp body, they slowly made their way down the gradual sloping ramp. The air now had a different feel to it. Fresher, due to being away from the stinking Tridon, and much cooler and pleasant as it hit their faces. Placing Zula carefully on the ground, the Evaders looked around, their eyes straining against the sudden darkness, hoping to see familiar faces at last.

Before they could do anything else, there was suddenly a deafening hissing sound and a cloud of yellow sulphuric steam emerged from the crashed ship. With a jolting loud movement against the rocky surface, the ramp began to disappear, reversing itself back into the noisy smelly ship, the doorway closed with a fast, circular movement until shutting tightly in the centre. With a loud rumbling sound and vibration which seemed to create a minor earthquake under the Evader's feet, the ugly ship violently shook and took off raising itself quickly up into the air, leaving a cloud of choking dust.

As fast as it had fallen, it disappeared up into the far away light above their heads, some several thousand feet up and then it was gone. What was left was a fresher smell of air and a relief on each of the Evaders faces. With a cheer, the Evaders jumped up and down excitedly. 'We have done it! We are safe. Home!' they yelled excitedly, as their sense of freedom had at last returned.

Little did the Evader friends know, that the escaped Tridon, was not just flying off to obscurity. As the ship chugged away at great speed, up over the snowy mountain range, further higher into the blue sky, and within minutes, reaching the edge of space, until only blackness outside eclipsed the ship.

As it headed off in the direction of the moon, beyond the other side, would be the gigantic Tridon mother ship, the size being as a small country on Earth, angrily waiting for news of the whereabouts of the escaped Evaders.

A few minutes more and planet Earth now out of sight, the Tridon ship reached its base, the most hideous monstrosity to grace the space airways, the mother ship resembled the look of a gigantic black shiny bug with enormous eyes watching in all directions. Through the enormous open mouth of the ship it flew, as if a tiny fish that was being swallowed by a giant whale. Then it closed its mouth and was gone.

The joy of the Evaders would be short lived.

'So, you think YOU are SAFE do you…?' Suddenly a booming deep voice emerged from the direction behind them. Looming out of the darkness, at first, came an angry pair of large eyes, the whites of them glowing in the dark. It was followed by a fierce face of shiny skin, its sweatiness highlighted further by the flickering glow from the torches sporadically placed around.

The large six feet five figure belonged to General Storm.

He had a look on his face as if he could no longer take any more humiliation from the Evaders. He was ready this time to explode.

The Evaders were too shocked to speak. They couldn't believe who was now standing in front of them; this had to be a cruel dream.

As the large figure loomed even closer towards them eclipsing their current four feet size statues, he was followed out of the darkness by a series of other military figures, maybe twenty or so, each carrying automatic weapons.

Behind them even further still, the Evader friends could begin to see their fellow Evaders slowly etching forward subserviently behind. As they cautiously wandered nearer, their voices could be heard, they appeared afraid and shaking. Most of them consisted of very young Evaders, some being only a tiny eighteen inches tall; the others appeared to be the most mature and wise ones, although lacking in the physical strength and agility they once had.

Overall, the remaining Evaders consisted of the most vulnerable of the population. The stronger ones however, were nowhere to be seen. Hundreds more, the younger agile ones were mysteriously gone.

General Storm loudly clicked together his enormous hairy fingers, as if rudely summoning an order. From behind the tall figures who shuffled awkwardly to one side, was a small but assertive looking Evader dressed in green, dwarfed by those standing around her. It was Electra! With a hard and unnecessary shove, Electra was pushed towards her friends who were so shocked but also relieved to see her again.

'Electra! It is you! You are safe!' Zeno said excitedly with a beaming smile and a big hug that swept Electra's feet off of the ground. The others too, hugged her. 'We thought you were dead!' Said Magenta. Electra shook her head with a smile, but then noticed Zula on the ground behind them lifeless and still.

Electra's mouth fell open with alarm 'I'm sorry, I'm sorry...' she stuttered with disbelief.

'Yes, we think so,' replied Fusion quietly, shaking his head. 'No more.'

The shock did not have time to set in, as General Storm's loud voice took over any emotions they needed to express at that moment.

Standing now just eight feet away from them, his voice and presence brought back the fear to them once more.

'Now you have had your cosy reunion, you'd better make the most of it. For your information, in case you wondered, your friends have gone looking for you! It's a pity they don't know that when they return empty handed, that on approaching this hideout, THEY WILL BE SHOT

DOWN!' he bellowed with a furious and contorted look on his face, as if pleased that he was once more in control.

'As for the rest of you, well, you'll be kept as specimens for experiments we need to carry out. They'll be no escape THIS time'

Before General Storm could continue any further, one of the other military officials went up to him, and promptly saluted.

'SIR! We have just had confirmation of alien ships approaching from a north easterly direction. Looks like them sir, and our missiles are at the ready...' General Storm rocked backwards and forwards on his heels, his large hands behind his back. 'Right. Don't fail me THIS time,' he boomed loudly. 'Position's at the ready!'

'YES SIR!' And with a salute, then turned to march off into the darkness, at the same time taking hold of the tiny microphone on the headset he was wearing, giving instructions for the military outside the volcano to be ready for the imminent attack, the missiles ready to fire. The Evaders were horrified and their alarmed voices and cries echoed around, they were helpless to do anything to help try to save the lives of their many friends whom unbeknown to them, were fast approaching to their imminent demise.

Chapter 35

'Get ready to fire!' came the order from Commander Bates through the headsets of the other fighter pilots who circled around high above, ready for the attack. What seemed to be a thousand or more alien ships fast approaching in the direction of the volcano hideout, their presence dominated the horizon as if a swarm of bees, a gigantic black wavering cloud.

As the alien swarm flew closer and closer, the snow covered mountain terrain below became engulfed in darkness, the sun being totally submerged from sight. Any wildlife below, the snow leopards included, all ran for cover, not understanding the sudden nightfall, and temperature falling as the sun disappeared, they were flying so close together, that electricity built up in between them creating small flashes of lightning.

It was also the deafening rumbling sound, as if like constant long rumbles of thunder as if a great storm was approaching.

Looking upwards you could see the almost black metallic of the alien ships resembling the underbellies of massive bugs. Each covered all over with what appeared to be black shiny bulbous eyes. You were being watched.

Captain Andy Rae was a most distinguished pilot, with much experience of air to air combat, but nothing he had ever witnessed before prepared him for what he saw.

'This is ECHO ONE. Do you copy we need back up, we need back up - NOW!' he yelled through his headset to the control air force base.

Captain Rae already realised it would take a minimum fifteen minutes flying time for back up to arrive and time already for them had run out. The black cloud now reached above the fighter pilots' heads. With the alien swarm approaching no more than twenty thousand feet up, the fighter pilots just had enough height to clear the highest mountain peaks below at some eighteen thousand feet. The distance between them didn't appear that much; they felt as if they were sandwiched in between two perilous hazards.

There came a further alarm now, as lightning bolts from the electricity charges from the Tridon ships above, began to strike down sporadically at the fighter jets, causing them to jump violently with each deafening impact. The Evaders at the bottom of the volcano knew that something up above wasn't right.

Zeno whispered in Magentas right ear. 'They cannot be Evaders up there coming towards us. We do not have that many ships…'

The other surrounding Evaders, including the most senior and younger ones, had overheard not only what Zeno had said but also on hearing from the aliens that thousands were approaching. The Evaders knew they only had about a dozen smaller ships at the most, and the other being the large carrier ship, but that was already parked up at the other side of the volcano base.

'What do you think is happening up there?' whispered Fusion looking back at the others. Electra shook his little shoulders.

'Perhaps they are not Evaders…'

'You alien things - QUIET back there!' Bellowed General Storm, deafening everyone inside the volcano as his shouts echoed around. The frustration was starting to get to him, not knowing what was clearly going on above his head and not feeling in control of the situation.

181

'Report to me. What is happening…' ordered the General, his face covered in sweat as he attempted to pull away the stiff collar and tie away from his broad neck.

Commander Bates listened intently again from Captain Rae's instructions.

'They say they need back up before they can fire. It's six against THOUSANDS!' stuttered the Commander, the panic evident in his voice.

Captain Rae radioed through to the other five pilots.

'Hold your fire. Commence stand-by positions. We wait for backup.'

'There won't be time for back up, do you copy?' replied echo four her voice appearing calmer.

There was no other choice for the pilots but to continue circling around, what was just two thousand or so feet underneath the mass entourage of the evil Tridon ships.

Suddenly, Captain Rae's worst fears were confirmed. Echo two flying at the same height and position just a hundred or so feet in front, exploded in a giant ball of flame, the shock wave jolting Captain Rae's seat in a sudden violent movement, the noise a sudden bolt of lightning.

The alien crafts above had already struck. Captain Rae and his good friend, now shaken by the unexpected explosion, saw the flaming debris of the jet plane fall almost in slow motion towards the mountain range.

'Echo three, four, five, six. This is echo one. Do you copy? Back to base! BACK TO BASE!' Captain Rae, the sweat now dripping from underneath his helmet, knew that their fire power against the evil ships above would be useless and their lives would be in vain. As he looked on either side of him, he could see with some relief, his crew disbanding, each turning steeply at a sudden sixty degrees angle, escaping the imminent danger.

However, as they suddenly manoeuvred and to his complete horror, both jets were simultaneously hit by luminous streaks of orange lightning, reaching their targets, exploding into giant balls of flame.

Echo three and four were also gone, the burning wreckage spiralling towards the snowy mountain range below.

'Echo five and six. DO YOU COPY?' Captain Rae's voice was impatient to hear an answer and began to shout his instructions. 'DO YOU COPY.?!'

'We're here, echo one. Heading for Charlie base…'

Now a sense of urgency crept over them.

'HEY! LOOK OUT!' suddenly from the righthand side high above Echo Five's head, an alien ship dispersed itself from the mass entourage above, swooping down at a steep angle towards the jet. Echo Five responded instantly by pulling away, in the effort to escape the fluorescent pulsating orange light about to emerge from the alien ship.

A huge explosion followed and much to the relief of Echo's one and six, they manage to see the pilot had ejected safely out, the parachute now gliding down towards the snowy capped mountain range directly below.

'Echo six. Do you copy?'

'Copy echo one. I've radioed through to base.

Bogey will be picked up.'

'Copy that. LET'S GET THE HELL OUT OF HERE!!'

As for the thousands of Tridons hovering in their ships above, they now only had one other target in mind - the volcano and the Evaders inside.

General Storm began pacing up and down, his large sweaty hands behind his back, his heavy boots making an uncomfortable grinding sound against the small rocks under his feet. He was very impatient for information.

'What is happening up there? Someone TELL ME!' He bellowed.

'Sir. I'm getting radio contact now…' replied Commander Bates, whose hand rested firmly against the ear piece on his headset, careful not to miss any information coming through from the fighter pilots above.

'Sir they see them, thousands… Outnumbered… Going to need reinforcements…' the Commander looked back up at General Storm, as if waiting to receive the next order. Only the remaining fighter planes circled above, waiting for the command to shoot.

Chapter 36

It wasn't long before the Tridons had a clear focus on the secret Evader hideout. The volcano had the most distinctive of shapes, dominant and proud, its 17,500-foot high perfect cone covered entirely in snow.

Looking below from their ships, the Tridons could see the centre of it, a massive black hole of nothing.

At the bottom of the volcano, General Storm's patience had run out.

Having just received the message from the radio call that the remaining fighter jets above had to abort their mission, angered him further still.

'Reinforcements are on the way, sir' informed Commander Bates, trying to ease the tension but the comment was returned with a steely look.

'If you want the job done properly - you have to do it yourself!' yelled the General loudly.

'But sir, they were dropping like flies up there...'

'I don't want EXCUSES!' the General bellowed, who then turned his back on his Commander and with big heavy strides, made his way towards the military helicopter that was parked up some fifty metres away.

When he reached the helicopter, he was horrified to see his pilot inside had fallen asleep, slumped over to one side against the door with a jacket that was rolled up and placed under his head!

To the amazement of the surrounding military personnel and the Evaders that followed, General Storm quickly pulled open the opposite side door of the helicopter, only then to slam it closed with such force and a loud bang, that echoed around the volcano. The helicopter pilot literally jumped out of his seat with such a fright, the look of terror so evident and his headphones were lying askew over his face.

General Storm slid open the side door once more, this time clambering into the seat alongside him, slamming the door shut.

'I suggest that if you want to KEEP your wings you stay AWAKE!' he roared, and his voice could be heard from those gathered around outside.

'Yes SIR!' the pilot replied, straightening up his headset.

'Take her up. I want to see what's going on out there!'

'Yes SIR!' the pilot responded subserviently and began to switch on the controls. The helicopter engine began to start up.

Both the Evaders and military personnel outside instantly shuffled back a safe distance from the huge blades that started to rotate.

With a high pitch whirl from the engine, everyone and everything outside the helicopter was being blown about, much to the amusement of the General whose face sneered against the window. Gently they started to rise up from the ground.

'Good bye. Don't come back!' shouted out Fusion at the top of his voice.

General Storm looked down below at those looking above at him. 'Morons,' he said. 'Totally useless.' The helicopter continued to rise now through the blackness of the surrounding volcanic walls. Only the front beam lights exposed them to any danger of the rotating blades colliding with the side, for as the higher they ascended, the surrounding cone shape grew gradually narrower and narrower.

General Storm glanced upwards towards the small circle of light high above them.

186

'Can't you go any quicker?' he moaned, turning to the pilot who was under extreme pressure anyway to control the helicopter under such dangerous circumstances. This time the pilot totally ignored him, concentrating hard.

Gradually the surrounding light around them became more natural, as they neared the uppermost part of the caldera.

General Storm looked up once more. 'Looks stormy out there, such a black sky,' he thought to himself, not realising the blanket mass of Tridon ships above were blocking out the sunlight.

Now they reached the upper most part of the volcano and as they looked straight ahead of them, they could see the surrounding snowy capped mountains, a spectacular sight. However, what they didn't notice was lurking above and behind them...

'How strange.' thought the General. 'It appears to be a lovely blue sky ahead, yet above us appears a fierce black cloud...'

The helicopter slowly swung round 180 degrees. Now they knew the answer why, for what seemed as far as they could see above them, was a huge mass of what looked like giant bugs, hovering in mid- air, as if a huge swarm of bees. For the first time ever, General Storm's mouth fell open. He was speechless. The pilot also, the look of horror on his face, he could also feel the instant hostile atmosphere, this terrifying sight now engulfing them.

As if in a moment of panic, the pilot took hold of the steering column, yanking it sideways and downwards as if wanting to escape, resulting in the helicopter suddenly beginning to spin out of control.

The General in his panic, outstretched his arms and legs as if grasping the nearest thing to hang onto, such was the speed at which it was now spinning.

'CONTROL... THIS... THING!' he yelled, terrified. The G Force of the spinning helicopter was so intense.

The pilot struggled to regain control, as the helicopter had other ideas. They continued spinning and falling at an angle towards the top edge of the snow-capped caldera. The Tridons watched from above, bemused and chuckling heavily to themselves, their bulbous stinking masses releasing clouds of yellow sulphuric gases.

The pilot was frozen in fear, realising his attempt to regain control where in vain, aware that the impact was inevitable.

With the helicopter still spinning and falling, he stared out of the window in front, almost as if in a trance, everything outside now was a blur; the white below them looming up fast and the blackness above them, the alien ships hovered, watching.

Arms and legs firmly outstretched in a panic, they both braced themselves for impact.

What felt as an enormous jolt, the helicopter slammed on the edge of the caldera, as it did so, turning violently to one side, the huge rotating blades buckling around them, flying off beyond and out of control.

The body of the helicopter itself, still intact, began rolling, rolling downwards towards the edge that would inevitably tumble them down the side of the volcano to meet their inevitable end. The side and front windows shattered.

The crumpled helicopter tumbled over the edge, at first the thick snow cushioning their fall and then the snow entering every area through the broken wreckage, almost with a sense of impending suffocation.

Now sliding out of control on its side, the shell of the helicopter headed straight for a raised snowy mound, being a large clump of rocks.

Suddenly there was an explosion, a huge ball of flame. General Storm was no more.

The Tridons hovering above in their ships continued to chuckle away, bemused at what they had just witnessed, further adding to their assumption that the aliens on this planet were not very bright or sophisticated at all.

The Tridons still being distracted by the unexpected helicopter crash, however, failed to notice themselves, what appeared to be a swarm of flying objects heading their way and coming up fast behind them!

The thousand or so strong swarm travelling some 2,000mph grew larger by the second, their intentions formidable and angry. They had only one purpose in mind.

The leader of the evil Tridons, whose ship was the most frightening and dominant looking amongst them, gave the order for the other tridon ships to attack the volcano site. Their intention would be to aim their lasers inside the caldera, inevitably creating an instant firestorm, killing all the Evaders and everyone inside. In its loud crackling voice, the Tridon leader ordered the ships nearest the volcano to counter fire their lasers. The countdown on the screens in front of them began: ><, ll>ll, ll>l, l>l, l>, >, llll, lll, ll, 1…

There was a tremendous explosion. It was such a deafening explosion, followed by a rumbling sound of the loudest thunder to be heard.

The target area was covered in a huge ball of orange flame, then creating a wide mushroom cloud as if being hit by an atomic bomb. The Tridons had been hit by a powerful mid- air cluster bomb, literally wiping out most of their entire ships, engulfing them in flame. In masses of twisted burning wreckage, the carnage fell towards the snowy mountain terrain below.

Now alarmed, the remaining Tridons turned their ships around to face this unexpected enemy, maybe a hundred or more fighter jets, now with more prepared destructive weaponry than before.

The enormous explosion shook everyone who was inside the volcano, the rocky walls and the ground beneath their feet shaking as if a serious earthquake had occurred. The air around them filled with particles of rocks and dust for a moment causing everyone to cough.

'What has happened out there?' choked one of the military personnel. Even he didn't know of the secret bomb that had been used outside.

'RADIO THROUGH SOMEONE!' shouted Commander Bates, who was next in authority, even if he looked shocked, his feet swaying unsteadily.

'It's that nasty alien up there,' announced Fusion, trying to stifle his coughs and waving his hands in front of him, in an attempt to clear the surrounding air.

'Perhaps it was the flying ship that the nasty alien was in, that crashed!' suggested Electra, looking pleased and thinking that she had guessed correctly.

'I know of no other alien to have the power to shake the ground like that.' said Zeno whose serious face was covered in rock dust.

'Only these aliens on this planet are different. These are a danger to themselves.'

Suddenly, there was another huge explosion, this time even more intense and louder than the last, violently shaking the Evaders and the military around so much so, that they were all thrown to the ground.

From all around them above their heads, rocks began to fall, some of which were the size of footballs, crashing down violently, narrowly missing the group of Evaders who were frantically rushing over to the edge of the walls in an attempt for protection.

The military personnel themselves were feeling very alarmed as to what was going on, on the outside. With their leader General Storm now gone and no information relayed to them from their radio calls, it was as if they themselves did not understand the situation that was occurring above them.

They had no control over what was happening. This was something new.

Commander Bates himself, crouching low on the ground, clutching his dust covered headset, repeated over and over again for any information that would update them of their situation.

'This is Commander Bates to Charlie base. Do you copy? We are in danger. REPEAT. WE ARE IN DANGER!' His voice grew louder and more impatient, the more times he tried. The only response he received from the frequency was a continuous crackling sound and only the faint unclear voice on the other end that could not be understood.

After a few long minutes of trying, the Commander gave up. 'It's no use,' he said despairingly to his personnel who now sat around feeling helpless.

They could only stare helpless back, their faces looking somewhat lost at what to do.

'It looks as if we are on our own...'

The prospect for survival for the humans and also for the group of young and old Evaders and the five Evader friends did not look good.

No contact now with the outside world. No ships left for them to fly off out into the unknown scene outside and the military helicopter gone.

They had no food, only trickling water from the melting snow that somehow had found a way inside the volcano, only to gather to a rock pool in the corner. This was not enough for any of them to survive for long. They had no escape.

Chapter 37

The Evaders and the now trapped and helpless soldiers, including the Commander, thought that whatever it was that was happening outside must be over. The past few minutes had after all been very quiet, apart from only distant rumblings. How wrong they were.

Two more enormous explosions followed, only a mere minute or so apart, even bigger than those before, again creating an earthquake 7.5 or more on the Richter scale.

Once again large rocks fell from above, crashing down with such ferocity, so narrowly missing those vulnerable below. However, they were unlucky to be hit by the smaller rocks that seemed to crash all around, which resulted in cuts and bruises for both the humans and the Evaders alike.

Zeno, Electra, Magenta and Fusion struggled as best they could to dodge the falling rocks at the same time, cowling over, in one corner, trying to protect Zula's lifeless form from any further injury.

Outside, the scene was nothing but sheer devastation.

What seemed to be the entire landscape, the once beautiful white, snow-covered mountains, was now covered in debris of twisted, burning wreckage. Most of the Tridon ships had been wiped out, a mass at a time, each mid- air cluster bomb dropped from high above, each atomic cloud had engulfed them to nothing. The Tridons were fighting a losing battle. The few that were remaining, returned enemy fire, their pulsating orange laser fire so often missing their targets unlike before.

Instead, now they were the ones left to be overpowered and shot down, many of them crashing, exploding into flame on the mountainsides below. Even the snowy capped volcano, before a dominating white beauty, its stunning slopes all around now covered in burning wreckage, melting the snow.

Some of the Tridon ships had crash-landed in one piece and although they were badly damaged and lay helplessly wedged in giant mounds of snow, the sulphur stinking Tridons inside were still alive.

The orders had been given for any surviving Tridons to be captured. This was much to the pleasure of General Storm's military replacement, now General Dragner, whose presence made the deceased Storm seem softer in nature by comparison. General Dragner however, gloated in his new victory, this was HIS success, no one else's, and he stood with his legs stood firmly apart in his military attire, rubbing his large hands together with glee, his bald white sweaty head glistening amongst the fluorescent coloured dim lights of the control room within the enormous Hercules plane that circled above the scene of the volcano.

'If those demon aliens are not rounded up within 1 hour- YOU'LL ALL BE DEMOTED TO PUSHING BROOMS!' he bellowed at the nervous personnel around him, who were saluting back with trembling hands.

'SIR! SIR! 'A member of radar control turned his head quickly over towards General Dragner, instantly grabbing his attention to something mysterious that suddenly appeared on the radar screens in front.

'WHAT!' stormed the General.

'Whatever it is sir, it is HUGE! Look at the speed it is going!

That can't be right!'

General Dragner stood mesmerized by the huge white cloudy mass that engulfed half the size of the monitor screen.

Whatever it was, it was approaching the volcano at incredible speed beyond that of human capability.

'Sir look. It is coming towards us! LOOK! There's another one! And ANOTHER sir!'

The General and everyone else stood around the screens with open mouths.

'Ask the flight deck if they can see anything!' he ordered. Then Lieutenant Penny rushed towards the flight deck, swiping the door open with her security card and then entered the pin number with a trembling hand.

Rushing into the flight deck with a nervous anticipation, the flight crew turned around quickly, eyes wide open with disbelief.

'ARE YOU SEEING THIS?' asked the Captain to the Lieutenant, then turning his head back towards the huge anomaly in the distance that seemed to be coming straight for them. Whatever it was, they were on a collision course.

'PULL UP! PULL UP!'

Chapter 38

The entire inside of the volcano began at first to vibrate gently, accompanied by what seemed a gentle humming sound. Then it got louder. Something on the outside was approaching, something BIG.

The Evaders now worn out with the thought of yet another possible violent event about to happen and the weariness was now beginning to show on their tired faces.

The group of military personnel looked almost as if in bewilderment at the Evaders. They knew it wasn't the familiar sound of approaching helicopters to the rescue. That was all they hoped for right now.

The small rocks on the ground began jumping around, moving by themselves such was the vibration, almost like a gentle rumbling earthquake, shook the volcano. The effect also shook their bodies through the hard rock surface beneath their feet and it became so bad, they had to stumble back up onto their feet with much reluctance.

'There's going to be another BANG!' said Fusion loudly, throwing his arms up in the air, echoing through the volcano walls, and not exactly reassuring the others around him.

'There is something up there...' said Magenta looking up transfixed.

'Something BIG!' said Electra demonstrating by holding both arms out as wide as she could.

'What is it Zeno?' Magenta asked, hoping for a reassuring answer.

'They are coming for us…' was all Zeno could say, looking upwards towards the circle of light high above them.

The other Evaders now also looked up, mesmerised, their bodies still shaking with the vibration. It was as if they were standing on top of a washing machine on spin dry.

The noise surrounding them, a loud humming sound now, began to paralyse them into a hypnotic trance.

All eyes continued to look up, the military also standing up amongst the Evaders at the sunlight so high above and then they noticed it. Very slowly it happened, whatever it was, it was large enough to cover the size of the top part of the caldera, gradually blocking out the small circle of sunlight as it swept across. The inside of the volcano grew steadily darker, all faces fading away in the darker light.

'They're here,' said Zeno loudly above the humming sound and vibration, but both his voice and face remained calm.

The others were glancing at Zeno for signs of reassurance.

'WHO'S here?' asked Fusion loudly.

Zeno did not answer and continued to stare upwards. 'It's the Tridons again. They are after you Fusion,' said Magenta.

The group of military personnel however started to feel very uneasy, now stepping back towards the walls edge of the volcano, as if not wanting to be part of whatever was going to happen.

The Evaders also feeling the tension in the air, began to pace backwards nearing the inside walls, there was a feeling of vulnerability all around them.

Suddenly, all eyes noticed movement above. The giant hovering space ship began to open in the middle, releasing what sounded like a high-pitched release of compressed air. What appeared to be an enormous circular platform began to lower itself downwards directly in the middle of the giant ship, right in the centre opening at the top of the volcano.

What the Evaders below and the few military persons could not see, was that on this platform that was lowering, was a smaller spaceship, circular in form with two tiers of smoothly curved metallic edges, immaculate and shinning brilliant silver in colour.

Unbeknown to those far below who watched transfixed, the alien ship gently rose from the platform, almost silently albeit for a gentle hum. For a moment it hovered as if waiting for instructions from those controlling, the ship glided to one side then came to a stop and hovered, now in full sight of those below. 'Here they come.' remarked Zeno calmly.

The military were now feeling alarmed and rushed to hide from this unknown alien presence, found themselves nowhere to hide, and instead clung to the sides of the volcanic walls with fear etched on their faces. For once they knew their weaponry was useless.

The alien craft was now about to add further to their panic, as very slowly, the hovering craft began to lower itself away from the huge ship above the volcano and slowly descended towards those gathered apprehensively below. Those watching could see the ship spiralling around as it graced itself further downwards, its size growing larger as it did so.

Now it was a mere hundred feet above their heads. The Evaders stood nervously, knowing that this alien presence would make itself known to all those who stood transfixed, watching. There was nowhere to run, nowhere to hide. Then it lowered itself further still, as it did so, creating a loud humming sound and in such a confined space that could only be endured by both the Evaders and the humans by covering their ears. As it continued to spin around so quickly, it was as if it was rotating around creating its lift. It produced a strong wind blowing the small frames of the Evaders almost off their feet.

Gradually the spinning slowed down, as it did so, the alien ship gently lowered itself onto the stony volcanic ground.

The loud humming sound softened until it completely stopped.

The ship now lay silent and still. Now a long minute had passed; no one on the outside said a word and no one moved. All eyes watched the craft, waiting for something to happen. The military personnel now feeling very uneasy with this new and unexpected presence drew their weapons at the ready.

They slowly began approaching the ship, their automatic weapons raised high and ready to fire on whatever it was that was inside.

Now their steps had reached the foot of the craft, the highest sides of which now towered some forty feet over their heads, they were now lost at what to do next.

They each looked at one another, but could only shake their heads or raise their shoulders. They didn't quite know what to do now.

Reluctantly, one of the soldiers was summoned to bang with their hand on the side of the craft. Intervention was needed.

Looking around at the others for a reassuring nod, the nervous looking soldier banged as loudly as he could on the side of the metallic alien ship, not realising it was covered in some sort of static electric charge creating a nasty shock. In pain and alarm, he jumped away. The soldier again banged on the side, creating another flurry of sparks and a yelp of pain.

Suddenly there was movement. The soldier now alarmed, almost tripped over his own feet as he turned and fled back towards the others. A high-pitched sound of compressed released air filled inside the volcano. Slowly a doorway emerged from the smooth curvaceous ship.

Zeno, Electra, Magenta and Fusion wandered closer towards it, their heads curiously turned to one side.

The other Evaders stood behind, nervously watching and waiting for the next sign of movement.

Inside the doorway was an expanse of darkness. Suddenly, what appeared to be a walkway to the ship emerged itself gracefully down at a slanting angle, and silently came to a halt on the rocky ground below.

The military personnel sensing hostile aliens about to emerge, aimed their automatic weapons at the ready, although each somewhat shaking with fear, with sweat pouring down their brows.

There was more movement. All those watching stepped back. Something began to emerge itself from the darkness.

As it slowly emerged, gasps drew from all those watching. They couldn't believe what they were seeing.

Chapter 39

Then from around the edge of the ship's entrance, it appeared. Slowly at first, almost inch by inch, until it thrust its large head out with enthusiasm for all those to see. Smiling at first, and with eyes large and bulging, it spoke.

'Going round in circles looking for you, don't you know!' the alien said, nodding away. The relief on the faces of the other Evaders could not be more obvious. With a ship now at their disposal, they were at last in a position to fly off to meet their freedom, away from the oppressiveness of their captors who just stood around staring in awe.

This was not exactly an everyday occurrence you would expect to see; an alien ship to arrive from nowhere with its inhabitant to show its face.

'Come, come…' The alien waved almost impatiently to the other Evaders who were still standing around almost in an amazed state and unsure as to what they should do next.

'Come, come, come…' the Evader repeated again, ignoring the military personnel who just stood with their mouths wide open and their weapons, although still clutching them, the barrels were facing downwards towards the rocky ground. There was a feeling of disbelief.

One by one, the reluctant group of Evaders edged forward very cautiously, nervous of any reaction from the towering military who stood transfixed, watching their every move. Their steps of sixty feet or so stopped as they reached the metallic walkway that had now descended gracefully to the ground.

Turning nervously around at their captors, the group of elder and young Evaders came to a stop before making any further step up the walkway to freedom.

Zeno, Electra, Magenta and Fusion were following, albeit slower as they carried Zula towards the ship. They too stopped, unable to proceed any further as their pathway was now blocked by the others who were nervously looking back.

The Evader, still at the entrance of the ship, started to grow impatient, not realising the danger the other Evaders below were facing. 'Move – move!' asked Fusion impatiently, clutching onto the lower parts of Zula's legs, ignoring the tension around him.

'You Evaders are so SLOW!' With that he began to edge further forward, nudging the others to one side. With Fusion now leading, a determined Zeno, Electra and Magenta followed, carrying the rest of Zula, whilst nodding at the others with anxiousness. Besides Fusion, they were feeling more wary of enticing a response from the military who up to now had been reluctant to make a hostile move, only due to their lack of leadership.

Now the four friends had reached the bottom slant of the walkway, with Fusion confidently leading, they began their gradual accent to the ship's entrance. Not once did Fusion look back. He was on a mission. The others however, were nervous. With every heavy step they took, they glanced back, almost preparing to be shot at any moment. Now the military, unsure of what to do, began shuffling awkwardly amongst themselves, looking at the next in charge. It was now Corporal Gracie, an indecisive and now looking slightly awkward military soldier, knowing the next order was going to come from him. 'Gracie – you're in charge! THEY'RE ESCAPING!'

His face now covered with sweat and his mop of blond hair now smothered in rock dust, the look of anxiousness etched on his face. Gracie then snapped out of his trance like state, suddenly realising his new responsibility.

'Positions ready. Get ready to aim…'

Having given the order that they had been waiting for, the soldiers automatically took their rigid stance, ready to fire on order, their eyes now transfixed on their targets. Almost in a straight line they stood, their barrels now facing the vulnerable looking elder and young Evaders who kept glancing back, sensing what was about to happen. The Evaders in their awkward shuffling way, stumbled so slowly up the ramp of the ship, many stopping to help those less strong and capable than themselves.

'Aim…' Corporal Gracie ordered. With each step they made, the Evaders looked back at their armed captors, now the fear etched clearly on their faces. They couldn't move faster if they tried. 'Aim…' ordered a reluctant Gracie louder still, about to initiate the final order.

Zeno and the others were still only halfway up the long ramp, now struggling with the weight of carrying Zula that was slowing them down.

Suddenly, Electra couldn't manage any longer and her arms had been stretching upwards for too long, her legs now heavily aching, and fell exhausted down onto the sloping ramp.

Zeno, Magenta and Fusion, still supporting the rest of Zula, lost momentum, and collapsed, also falling onto the sloping ramp, now all of them beginning to slide back down again where they had started.

Sweaty fingers now tightly poised holding their weapons, they were ready to fire with each one firmly fixed on their easy targets just thirty feet away.

Corporal Gracie's face, now even more sweaty, his eyes also transfixed on the large group of fallen Evaders, his mouth braced open, ready to give the order. The Evaders all looked back at him, their big eyes all told him everything he knew - they sensed they were about to meet their fate.

'FIRE.!!'

Within a split second of the command being made, the ships lights suddenly blazed on so brilliantly, that all eyes wide and focused on the Evaders were instantly blinded. In cries of pain, the soldiers clasped the palms of their hands over their eyes. The white blazing lights of the ship totally blinded them, bringing them to their knees.

The Evaders, still piled up in a heap at the bottom the ramp, had been fortunate at the time to have their eye's tightly closed waiting to be shot.

It was only the quick thinking of the Evader inside the ship who realised what was about to happen and promptly decided to turn on the ship's lights on full beam, then turning them off after a few blinding seconds.

"EVADER'S! QUICKLY! Let's move, before they wake up again!" ordered Zeno to the others around him, who were still lying in a shocked and collapsed state.

"Will you get OFF OF ME!" Fusion moaned loudly to Magenta who had slid on top of him almost face to face, then firmly pushed Magenta back off. "Your breath smells ANYWAY!" Magenta huffed back, clambering awkwardly up to her feet again ready to help Zula again up the ramp.

"Electra – quickly – MOVE!" Zeno now panicked on noticing Electra lying against the shoulder of another Evader at the side of the ramp.

"The aliens are coming for us! QUICKLY!" Panic now set in, as the soldiers, still shielding their eyes, began to clamber to their feet. "CAN'T SEE!" one of them said distressingly. "I'M BLIND!"

"Where are they!" yelled another, whose eyes were screwed up and watering, the frustration evident on his face as he clambered back onto his feet, and started pointing his automatic rifle in all directions. "I'LL GET THEM!" another yelled, also clambering back up to his feet, only then to trip over his heavy awkward army boots and fall back onto the ground.

In a split second without any hesitation, Zeno, Electra, Fusion and Magenta each fired their Glugers, ejecting the powerful resin from their weapons, instantly paralyzing the enemy.

"EVADERS – QUICKLY! Back into the ship!" ordered Zeno with loud desperation to the many others who were still too slow trying to move up the crowded ramp. Zeno started to follow them, supporting Zula's shoulders on either side along with Magenta, whilst Electra and Fusion struggled supporting her legs, their strength and stamina being tested to the limits whilst trying to walk up the sloping ramp of the ship.

"QUICKLY!" Zeno prompted the others who desperately appeared to be lagging behind.

"FIRE!" Yelled out Fusion loudly to Zeno and the others, who responded by instantly firing their Glugers with one hand, whilst struggling to support Zula's weight with the other.

Bullets flew in all directions; the firepower was intense.

The Evaders fired with all their power, managing to disable most of the remaining soldiers who were firing back at them, the bullets ricocheting off the volcanic walls and the side of the spaceship in the hope of destroying the Evaders.

The noise from the constant firing from both sides, was deafening.

A few of the soldiers were desperately trying to clamber up the ramp of the ship. A few lucky Evaders had managed to scramble their way to the safety of the ship, disappearing into the darkness beyond.

The others however, including Zeno and Magenta who were also struggling half way up the ramp, found it difficult gaining momentum. Both Electra and Fusion in their rush, kept dropping to their knees. The combination of constant firing in all directions both from them and the enemy, along with the weight of Zula had become too much. Although determined to move much faster to safety, their legs were straining under the pressure.

With what remaining strength and courage they had, Zeno and Magenta pulled Zula along, so determined to reach the entrance of the ship. Just thirty more feet and safety would be theirs, but as they pulled, both Fusion and Electra lost their grip.

They immediately fell backwards onto the sloping ramp. This time they were even more vulnerable to the bullets that were flying in all directions. In the panic to reach the doorway and escape to safety, the other Evaders began clambering over Electra and Fusion, smothering them. The many hands and feet of Evaders now engulfed them to the point that even their faces were buried under the chaos.

Zeno and Magenta however, had finally managed to reach the doorway, placing Zula safely, just inside the entrance of the ship, but as they then turned around, they couldn't see their friends any longer. All they could see was a chaotic scene of the frightened faces of many panicking very young and elder Evaders scrambling to safety. Up until now, the bullets had ricocheted off of everything else – the Evaders had been lucky.

The soldiers now in their blind determination continued to fire and they could almost sense the direction now of where the Evaders were, as they could hear them.

The soldiers one by one, began edging forward and although still temporarily blinded, their confidence grew as their hearing and senses became stronger. The hostile aliens had located their targets.

Suddenly, Electra yelled loudly in pain. She had been hit. Now tightly clutching the upper part of her injured thigh, blood began to appear through under her stretched out hand. Zeno and Magenta looked on in horror and the feeling of being powerless was unbearable. Electra, now buried under two collapsed Evaders, felt paralysed at not having the strength to push them off. The relentless firing then suddenly stopped.

"CEASE FIRING! RE – LOAD MAGAZINES!" Came the loud order from Corporal Gracie, as slowly one by one, the soldiers' eye sights began to recover. They started stumbling around and rubbing their eyes as if they had just woken from a sleep.

Now more panic set in for the remaining Evaders who were alive, to try to scramble to safety but most had either been shot like Electra, or like Fusion unable to move due to them being weighed down by fallen Evaders. As quickly as they could, Zeno and Magenta began to make their way hastily back down the ramp. "QUICKLY Magenta! They will start to shoot again!" As they reached their friends, they began desperately pulling at their arms.

"It's no use!" cried out Electra, staring upwards at Magenta. "I can't MOVE!" Just as Zeno tried to free Fusion from under the many fallen Evaders, Fusion's face was now appearing shocked.

Wondering why Fusion looked alarmed, Zeno turned around.

The soldiers, their eyesight now regained and their composure restored, now stood poised and ready once more to fire upon them.

The Evaders were trapped and they knew that they would not be able to move quickly enough to escape the gunfire.

'EVADERS! POWER AS ONE.!!' Cried out Zeno to the others in a loud voice of defiance. As they each lay trapped on the ramp of the ship under the weight of the other collapsed Evaders, the four friends somehow managed to stretch out each of their arms, firmly gripping their Glugers from their belts, uniting their Glugers together, creating a powerful force.

Excited and newly charged with energy, the Evader's now promptly stood up, holding each of their own Glugers high above their heads, which firmly touched together in a gleaming silver pyramid of brilliant light. The Planet Evaders repeated together:

'POWER AS ONE!'

Within the blinding white flash of light, they were instantly transformed from their petite 4ft tall frames, to 7ft tall strong and athletic statues of muscle and agile power. The Planet Evaders now stood proud and imposing, their feet now stood apart in a powerful stance, ready to pounce with bounding new energy upon their hostile enemy.

On witnessing this sudden transformation, Corporal Gracie gave the orders.

"… AIM YOUR WEAPONS…!" he bellowed.

"AIM…Keep your rifle still – PRIVATE SPEDDING before I point that weapon at you MYSELF!" shouted Corporal Gracie on noticing one of them falter under the pressure.

With bounding new energy, the Evaders leapt from the high ramp of the space ship onto the ground with a heavy thud, their Glugers firing the paralyzing extract, instantly disabling the attacking enemy, as they collapsed onto the ground, wrapped tightly in epoxy resin.

Suddenly, the Evaders could feel a tremor from under their feet. They realised that the ship behind them was about to take off without them, as it began to start powering up!

Zeno shouted to the others – 'QUICKLY.! RUN TO THE SHIP.!!'

With bounding giant strides of energy, the Evaders leapt up onto the tall walkway of the large space ship, just managing to catch the last remaining section, as it disappeared swiftly into the side of the ship's entrance.

The doors of the ship appeared to evaporate, no door lines in sight, leaving just a smooth metallic silver shell on the outside, much to the amazement of the military who looked up in awe.

Startled, the remaining few soldiers with their weapons still poised for attack, looked just as shocked as Corporal Gracie who didn't react quickly enough to what just happened, their opportunity now gone.

Suddenly, a loud humming sound filled the air, loud enough for the soldiers to have to cover their ears. The ship now gently rose upwards, as it did so, its smooth rounded silver shell began rotating, creating a wind inside the volcano as if a helicopter taking off.

Choking dust filled the air once more, the soldiers now having to shield their eyes not wanting to incur any more damage to themselves. Then as the ship gathered more height, the dust that flew everywhere and the loud humming sound gradually decreased to nothing.

Corporal Gracie, so angry and frustrated at himself for delaying his command to destroy the Evaders, his only chance for notoriety gone, stared up along with the others. Now they were all helpless and stranded.

The bottom of the alien ship displayed an array of fluorescent lights of bright orange, green and red, rotating around creating its powerful energy. Just a few seconds more, and the ship rose out from the enormous caldera, its smooth silver shell glistening against the late sun.

The Evaders inside were now safe from the evils on the outside, each one safely cupped in huge water filled seats that moulded the contours of their bodies. The surrounding light was of warm apricot, a reassuring ambience.

The Evader medical crew were aboard, tending to those that needed urgent care, administering powerful tonics to take the pain away, almost sending them to sleep until they reached the medical centre on board the main ship where they were heading.

Zula had already received priority treatment and had even slowly started to recover and wake, much to the relief of the others who looked anxiously on. Her injuries were treatable, and her grey complexion now replaced with a healthier warmer glow. Electra also, was given a strong tonic of medicine for the pain, now sending her to sleep.

Zeno, Magenta and Fusion, their powerful strong frames had now returned to their normal smaller size, sat almost cocooned back in their seats side by side, relieved to not feel threatened anymore.

"I used to look up at the stars from our own planet, wondering what was out there, wanting adventure," Remarked Zeno gaining attention from the others. "Now all I wish was that I was back at home." Fusion sat covered head to toe in bruises, interrupted. "You always want what you cannot have!" he replied.

"We should have left Fusion behind with the Tridons!" replied Magenta. "He alone would have scared them off!"

Suddenly the sound of snoring interrupted their conversation. Electra was curled up fast asleep but at least when she awakes, she will not experience danger as she had before and there was a look of contentment on her face. "We are all safe now Electra," whispered Zeno.

The ship continued to fly upwards.

Above them, were the three huge Trillion ships, patiently hovering over the mountain range. The nearest had already prepared for the landing of the ship, its huge platform descended below it, as if it were a landing strip in mid- air.

There was a sudden jolt as the ship docked, then rose itself upwards. Now there was a hype of activity as Evaders started to move in all directions, ready to transfer those injured including Zula, to the main medical area.

Zeno and the others couldn't understand where the ships that disappeared had come from. All the Evaders aboard were presumed shot down and dead.

"Where did you go.?" asked Zeno to the first Evader who approached his huge comfy seat, helping him up. The Evader looked back and smiled.

"After our other Trillion ship was shot down and your ship had no other choice but to land, we managed to escape. We had to submerge our ships in the sea beyond, many depths below with the strange creatures watching us. We flew off under the sunlight each day to recharge our solar energy, storing it for the next journey ahead."

At last, the Evaders had a chance to rest.

The three huge Trillion ships, with their friends now safely aboard, gradually rose up into the early evening pink sky as the sun was setting.

On the horizon beyond the mountains, the beautiful orange sun was finally setting, leaving behind yet another day.

This planet wasn't the safe and friendly environment as the Evaders had hoped to find.

Now it was their mission to source a new home elsewhere.

Off the ships flew up into the starry night sky above, passing the moon as they went, with a universe ahead of them yet to explore.

Little did the Evaders know that as the Trillion ships flew passed the moon, that their unknown journey deep into space would be followed...

Printed in Great Britain
by Amazon

84003801R00122